"I have a solution to our little problem," Connor said.

"What sort of solution?" Jasmine wondered.

Again he let the silence continue unbearably. "The sort of solution that will dispel all the rumours and restore family faith in the two miscreants."

"A miracle?" she asked, with a rueful edge to her voice. She heard him chuckle again.

"Not quite a miracle, but an amazing occurrence for all that."

"What?"

"Marriage."

"Marriage?" She almost choked on the word. "Whose marriage?"

There was an infinitesimal pause.

"Our marriage…"

Legally wed,
But he's never said...
"I love you."

They're

Wedlocked!

The series where marriages are
made in haste...and love comes later....

Watch for more books in the
popular WEDLOCKED! miniseries

Coming next month:
His Bride for One Night
by Miranda Lee
#2451

Coming in April:
The Billion-Dollar Bride
by Kay Thorpe
#2462

Available only from Harlequin Presents®

Melanie Milburne

THE AUSTRALIAN'S MARRIAGE DEMAND

Wedlocked!

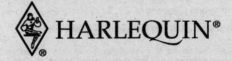

HARLEQUIN®

TORONTO • NEW YORK • LONDON
AMSTERDAM • PARIS • SYDNEY • HAMBURG
STOCKHOLM • ATHENS • TOKYO • MILAN • MADRID
PRAGUE • WARSAW • BUDAPEST • AUCKLAND

To Phil,
my second-born son, who constantly astounds me
with his intellect and wit and inbuilt talent for cynicism.
This one's for you, Phil!

ISBN 0-373-12449-X

THE AUSTRALIAN'S MARRIAGE DEMAND

First North American Publication 2005.

Copyright © 2004 by Melanie Milburne.

This edition published by arrangement with Harlequin Books S.A.

® and TM are trademarks of the publisher. Trademarks indicated with
® are registered in the United States Patent and Trademark Office, the
Canadian Trade Marks Office and in other countries.

www.eHarlequin.com

Printed in U.S.A.

CHAPTER ONE

IT WAS not quite light when Jasmine woke in the hotel bed.

She opened one sleepy eye and wondered what had wakened her. Perhaps it had been one of the wedding guests coming in late after a full night of partying, she thought, as she stretched out one cramped leg.

It had been a nice enough wedding as far as weddings went.

Her sister Sam had looked beautiful and happy, and Finn, Sam's new husband, had been glowing with pride, his handsome face wreathed in smiles all day and most of the night.

Her father had beamed down at everyone proudly from the pulpit of the Sydney suburban cathedral where he was the local bishop. He was pleased that he'd yet again been privileged with the honour of marrying another of his four daughters; her mother had dabbed at her eyes repeatedly and played the role of mother of the bride with thrice-practised aplomb.

It was a pity Finn's older stepbrother, Connor Harrowsmith, had to be the best man, but he'd more or less behaved himself, which was unusual, Jasmine reflected. He'd fulfilled his duties, producing the rings at the right moment, without mishap, even complimenting the three bridesmaids with no sign of his usual mocking humour until his dark brown gaze had singled her out. She'd smiled back sweetly, determined not to let anything or anyone spoil her sister's day, but inwardly she'd seethed.

She hated him and he knew it.

She could tell from the hard glitter that came into his eyes every time he looked at her, which was rather too often throughout the service and reception. It had been as if he were silently teasing her, the words filling the air between them even though he hadn't said a word: three times a bridesmaid never a bride. She had heard it in her head each time his dark eyes had sought hers and she resented him for it.

Jasmine stretched her other leg and froze.

There was someone in the bed with her!

She held her breath, wondering if she should turn on the lamp but too frightened to do so in case it woke whoever was beside her. She edged herself away as carefully as she could, but even when she was practically hanging over the edge of the mattress she could still feel the warmth of the stranger's body as if it was reaching out to draw her back into the co-coon of the bed.

The room was cloaked in darkness, a darkness that was suddenly menacing.

She could hear the sound of rhythmic breathing, the slight rustle of the bedclothes as the stranger moved, stretching, reaching out hands to find her...

She leapt for the light switch and snapped it on, her eyes shrinking painfully as the bright glare filled the hotel room.

'Oh my God!' she gasped. *'You!'*

She stared in horror when she saw Connor Harrowsmith, his long, muscled body clearly outlined by the bedclothes straining against the hard male form lying beneath.

'Hello, Jasmine,' he drawled. 'Did you sleep well?'

She drew in a furious breath as she grabbed the hotel bathrobe to cover her near nakedness. Her matching bra and panties had cost a fortune but there was no way he was going to get a free peep show!

'Get out of my room!'

He arched one dark sardonic brow as he rolled on to his side to face her, the sheet falling away from his naked chest revealing a rock hard stomach, the ridges of muscle clearly visible.

'Your room?'

'Of course it's my room; now get out before I call Security.' Her eyes flew to where her suitcase should be but, to her shock, it wasn't there.

'Where are my things?' She glared at him.

'In your room.' He stretched again, which pulled the sheets even tighter across his pelvis.

Jasmine tore her eyes away and stormed towards the bathroom. She wrenched open the door but there was no sign of the neat little row of cosmetics she had left the afternoon before; instead there was an electric shaver, a bottle of expensive-looking aftershave, a male hairbrush and, to add insult to injury, a wet towel on the floor.

She stomped back out to the bedroom, her anger increasing at the sight of him propped up lazily against the pillows, his taunting gaze slowly moving over her.

'You've taken my things!' she accused, moving towards the bed to reach for the phone. 'I'm going to call Reception and have someone sent up to—'

A large male hand appeared over her wrist, the long fingers encircling the slender bones in a gentle but undeniably firm hold.

'I wouldn't if I were you,' he cautioned, his dark eyes meeting hers.

'Let me go.' She tested his hold but it remained firm.

'You'd look really silly complaining to management when actually it's you in the wrong room,' he said.

'I'm not in the wrong room,' she insisted. 'I used my key in the lock last night.'

'I didn't lock the door,' he said. 'I left the reception to dash up here to get something I'd promised Finn and forgot to lock it on the way out.'

'I don't believe you.'

He shrugged indifferently and let her hand drop. She rubbed at it furiously, not because he'd hurt her but more to take away the sensation of his warm fingers.

'Go and see for yourself,' he challenged her. 'Open the door and check the room number.'

Jasmine swung away and padded over to the door with a confidence that was visibly cracking. What if he was right?

What if she was in the wrong room? How would she live that down?

She opened the door and her heart sank when she saw the number. She was in the wrong room! And not just any wrong room—Connor Harrowsmith's room!

'All right.' She walked back in, her colour high. 'So I made a mistake, but that still doesn't explain why you got into this bed without telling me of my error.'

'I didn't want to wake you,' he said, his tone guileless.

'Oh, for God's sake!' she fumed. 'You had no right to take advantage of the situation!'

He propped his hands behind his head, his biceps bulging, as did Jasmine's eyes at the sheer size of their gym-toned strength.

'How do you know I took advantage of the situation?' he asked with a long leisurely slide of his dark eyes all over her outraged form.

She felt flustered and over-hot, as if he'd flicked a switch on her body while she'd slept, turning her usual cool control to a completely different setting.

She didn't know what to think.

How was she supposed to know what had happened during the night? He might have touched her for all she knew and she'd be none the wiser. Perhaps he'd even kissed her, stroked her breasts or…

'You snore, you know,' he said, interrupting her torturous thoughts.

'I do not!'

His eyes twinkled as he surveyed her outraged features. Her curly chestnut hair was looking very 'just out of bed' and her grey-blue eyes were flashing fire. Notwithstanding the delightfully clingy ice-blue bridesmaid's dress she'd worn the day before, he couldn't think of a time when she'd looked more beautiful.

'Come on, Jasmine,' he teased. 'Loosen up. You're safe with me.'

'No one with a pulse is safe with you,' she tossed back irritably.

He laughed and threw the bedcovers aside.

'What are you doing?' she shrieked.

'Getting out of bed.' He stood up.

She turned the other way so she didn't have to look at his naked maleness. Her breathing was hurried and shallow, her face aflame, her nerves stretching like tight wires underneath her pulsing flesh.

'For God's sake put something on!' she croaked.

'You're wearing my bathrobe,' he pointed out dryly.

She seriously considered giving it back to him. Anything was better than having to face such a blatant show of male flesh in its prime.

'I haven't anything to wear.' Her voice was hoarse.

She felt his smile as he drawled, 'The eternal female lament.'

She heard a rustle of fabric. Then, out of the corner of her eye, she saw her bridesmaid's dress sail through the air towards her.

'Here, put this back on,' he said. 'I'll turn my back.'

She knew he was still looking at her as she let the bathrobe slip. She didn't trust a word that came out of that sensual mouth but she wasn't brave enough to turn and check. She struggled into the blue dress and, once she was decently covered, tossed the bathrobe in his direction without turning around.

'You can turn around now,' he said.

She turned around cautiously and his eyes met hers. She was relieved to see the bathrobe covered him but it gave her a funny feeling to think that minutes before the soft white folds had been lying against her own skin and now they were lying intimately against his.

'I have to go.' She headed for the door, almost tripping over her own feet.

'Hey,' he called as she fumbled with the door knob. 'Aren't you forgetting something?'

'What?' She gave him a glance over her left shoulder.

He held up one long finger where her pair of strappy sandals dangled.

'Oh.' She let the door go and approached him. 'Thank you.' She went to snatch them out of his hold but his hand caught hers.

His dark eyes burned down into hers.

'I enjoyed sleeping with you.' His thumb began stroking along the underside of her wrist in slow, sensuous strokes that made her stomach give a sudden unexpected lurch.

She found it hard to hold his gaze.

'I hope I didn't disturb you too much,' she said, making an effort at lightness.

'Oh, you disturbed me a great deal,' he said, giving her wrist a little tug. 'A great deal indeed.'

She was up against him, her body pressed to his, her softness on his hardness. She felt the outline of his growing erection against her belly and her eyes widened in alarm.

'Please—' her plea was breathy and ragged '—let me go.'

'You didn't say that last night.'

Her eyes widened even further.

'What do you mean?'

His eyes gave nothing away.

'You were quite the little temptress.'

She felt sick with shame. Had she really? Had she? Oh, dear God, had she thrown herself at him? But, deep down, she was fairly sure she hadn't.

'I don't believe you.'

'Oh ye of little faith,' he goaded.

'You're making it up to poke fun at me,' she said.

'Now why would I do that?'

'Because you're an arrogant jerk who thinks every woman will automatically fall into your arms, that's why.'

'That's an interesting analysis of my character, but not exactly true.'

'Isn't it?' Her look was cynical.

'You've been reading too many gossipy magazines,' he said. 'Don't you know they make it up to fuel their readership?'

'Everything you do is news,' she pointed out. 'You deliberately court scandalous gossip just to annoy your stepfather.'

His eyes hardened and his hold on her arm tightened a fraction.

'Just because your sister managed to get her hooks into my stepbrother doesn't mean you get the right to comment on the affairs of my family.'

'I can say what I like,' she tossed back defiantly.

'Not without paying a price.'

'What price?' A tiny shiver of apprehension shimmied its way up her spine.

'This price,' he said and, bending his head, captured her mouth with his.

She should have fought him.

She knew she should, but her body wasn't listening to the frantic plea of her brain. It was as if her body was acting totally independently of all rational thought and reason, going on its own wilful way, relishing the feel of a very male mouth commandeering hers.

His tongue pushed her trembling lips apart and sank into her mouth, searching for her own tongue. He found it and played with it tantalisingly, drawing it into the heat of his own mouth. Jasmine could feel the liquefying impact on her legs and spine as she leant against him for support, certain that without it she'd slip to the floor in a pool at his feet. His arms were like bands of iron, drawing her even closer, making her irrevocably aware of his aroused body against the trembling weakness of hers.

The kiss went on and on. She was lost to the feel of his lips exploring the soft contours of hers, lost to the sensation of hot desire flooding her internally as if all her life she'd been waiting for this moment.

He lifted his head and she blinked open her eyes.

'You shouldn't have done that,' she said.

'Nor should you.' His eyes glinted with some indefinable emotion.

'I didn't do anything!'

'Yes, you did.' He grinned at her wolfishly. 'You kissed me back.'

'I...I...' There wasn't much she could say in her own defence. 'You caught me off guard. I was unprepared.'

'I'll have to remember that,' he said. 'It might be useful.'

She wrenched herself from his arms and flung herself towards the door, unconcerned that her shoes were still in his possession. She opened the door of his room and had only taken one step out into the corridor when a camera flash blinded her.

'What the—?' She held up her hands to her face but the camera flashed three more times.

She elbowed her way past the persistent photographer and quickly dashed to her room, opening it with trembling fingers and slamming the door behind her as if it were the devil himself she was trying to lock out.

She took several deep breaths as she leant her back against the door, trying to calm her over-stretched nerves.

Damn him! How dared he mock her? Connor had probably organised the press to be waiting outside the door to get the scoop of the week. She inwardly cringed when she thought about her father reading the news of his daughter's latest misdemeanour. Her mother would no doubt retreat to her room with a cold face-cloth over her face, mortified that yet again she'd have to face the other women at Tuesday morning's Bible group with her wayward daughter's exploits as the main focus of study.

Her three sisters would frown and shake their heads, each of them looking towards their successful husbands for emotional support as they faced yet another of their sister's scandals.

She pushed herself away from the door and began packing her things. She didn't bother to fold anything; she just shoved everything in viciously as if each and every item was a piece of Connor Harrowsmith's anatomy she wanted to injure.

She hated the way he mocked her. Every time she'd met him during the course of her sister's friendship and subsequent courtship with Finn she'd had to bear the brunt of his ridicule. She knew she was an easy target given her tarnished reputation but she resented him for latching on to it so assiduously. Her name had been dragged through the mud on more occasions than she cared to recall, each time damaging the high moral ground of her family's home.

She thrust her cosmetics haphazardly into a plastic bag.

OK, so she wasn't technically a virgin. So what? She bet her sisters hadn't exactly made it to the altar intact but she didn't hear anyone complaining, least of all her parents.

She'd never been able to please them.

No matter what she did, it upset their strict idea of what was good and proper. Of course her work at the drug centre in Sydney didn't help but she wasn't giving that up for anyone.

She slammed her suitcase shut and scowled at her reflection in the mirror above the dressing table.

No matter how hard she'd tried to fit in she'd never quite managed to cope with the stultifying existence of being the eldest of Bishop Byrne's daughters, all dressed up in their Sunday best, sitting in the church pew, their undivided attention on the erudite wisdom spouting forth from their father's mouth, droning on like a blowfly stuck in a milk bottle.

No, Jasmine had sat and squirmed in her seat for as long as she could remember. She'd hated the dour music and the way all of the women had tried to out-dress each other every week. She'd hated the way the Sunday School teachers frowned at her questions and talked behind their hands in reproving conspiracy at her wilful disobedience. She'd walked out of the gargoyle-appointed cathedral at the age of sixteen and had never looked back, except in anger. In anger at the way her choice of belief system had alienated her from her parents even as they preached tolerance and acceptance.

Jasmine hadn't even seen a copy of Monday morning's paper when her second youngest sister called her on the telephone.

'How could you do this?' Caitlin cried.

Jasmine stiffened in preparation for the damning tirade.

'After all you've put us through, you do this, as if that affair with Roy Holden wasn't enough!'

'I didn't have an affair with—'

'How could you sleep with Connor Harrowsmith? How could you? You know what he's like; Finn is always telling us about his playboy exploits.'

'I didn't exactly sleep with—'

'Of course Father is beside himself. The Archbishop has already called this morning and now Mother has a migraine and it's entirely your fault.'

Jasmine let her sister run herself out. There was no point in stating her case. No one would believe her if she tried, but her anger and resentment towards Connor increased by several notches.

'I just hope Samantha and Finn don't look at this morning's paper,' Caitlin continued. 'Otherwise their honeymoon is going to be completely spoilt by your foolish and reckless behaviour.'

Jasmine had heard enough.

'If Finn and Sam are reading the paper on the second day of their honeymoon then Finn isn't half the man he should be,' she said.

Caitlin's gasp was clearly audible.

'You're so shameless! How can you be so flippant? At least Finn has some sort of morals, unlike his wayward, philandering stepbrother.'

Strange though it seemed, Jasmine suddenly felt compelled to spring to Connor's defence.

'You hardly know the man,' she said. 'It's not fair to judge.'

'Not know him? Everyone knows him. Every movement he makes is splashed across the papers all the time. He's Sydney's biggest playboy and you were photographed half-dressed coming out of his room the morning after your sister's wedding.'

'I wasn't half-dressed,' Jasmine said more calmly than she felt. 'I just didn't have my shoes on.'

'And where were they?' Caitlin's tone was snide. 'Still underneath Connor Harrowsmith's bed?'

She didn't bother denying it.

'They were in his possession, yes.'

'I can't believe you can be so casual about this!'

'I'm not being casual.'

'Well, you won't be when you hear what Father has said.'

'What?'

'Father is outraged. He's threatening to prosecute Connor if he doesn't do something to immediately quell the scandal.'

'It's hardly a scandal—'

'You might like to remind yourself at this point that our father is a prominent member of the clergy. *This* is a scandal!'

'I think it's more of a scandal when people stick their noses into business that has absolutely nothing whatsoever to do with them,' Jasmine replied. 'I've got to go to work. Goodbye.'

She hung up the phone and fumed.

Damn him! This was entirely his fault!

The telephone rang again and she stared at it for a long moment before picking it up. The last thing she wanted was a tearful how-could-you-do-this-to-us-after-all-we've-done-for-you type of conversation from her distraught mother. Nor could she currently cope with a condescending, moralising lecture from her 'holier than thou' father.

'If you're ringing to criticise me then hang up right now,' she said into the receiver.

'I wasn't calling to criticise you.' Connor Harrowsmith's deep voice sounded in her ear.

Her hand tightened around the receiver.

'I take it you've seen the morning papers?' she asked.

'Have you?'

'Not as yet but I've been informed of their content.' Her tone was bitter. 'It seems I'm in the middle of yet another scandal, this time with you as my partner in crime.'

'Poor you.' He laughed. 'To have sunk so low.'

'This isn't funny!' she raged. 'This is all your doing.'

'I accept total responsibility.'

She frowned. 'What do you mean?'

'As you say, it's all my fault.'

Jasmine didn't think he sounded at all contrite; on the contrary, he sounded rather proud of the fact that he'd caused so much of a scandal.

'My father is furious,' she put in.

'So is my stepfather.'

'And my mother has a headache,' she added.

'I shouldn't wonder, having to listen to your father's sermons all the time.'

She opened her mouth to attack him but changed her mind.

'My sisters will probably never speak to me again,' she said instead.

'So?' She could almost sense his dismissive shrug. 'When was the last time they listened to what you had to say?'

She hated to allow him to be right but he was. Even as she privately marvelled at his insight into the dynamics of her family, another part of her still wanted to fight him.

'My family are very important to me,' she said.

'How admirable of you.'

'You're making fun of me.'

'No. I'm actually on your side in all this.'

'I don't believe you.'

'I can see why your father has such an issue with you,' he said wryly. 'Your lack of faith is lamentable.'

'You're making fun of me again.'

He laughed.

'Maybe I'm poking fun at life in general. Don't take it too personally.'

'Is your stepfather threatening to disinherit you too?' she asked.

'He shouldn't,' he said. 'I didn't do anything wrong.'

'You slept with me,' she said. 'Deflowering a bishop's daughter is pretty high up on the unforgivable sins chart.'

'But you're not the innocent virgin, are you?' he said.

Jasmine wasn't sure how to answer him. The papers had been full of her 'inappropriate relationship' with Roy Holden; Connor surely could not have been unaware of that. But while the press loved a scandal, they were less particular over the truth, and that lay within her, untouched.

'According to popular opinion I'm an "outright tart",' she quoted.

'I've never been one for popular opinion,' he said. 'I like to find out these sorts of things for myself.'

Jasmine felt a funny sensation rush through her at the thought of him examining her intimately. She dismissed the thought and schooled her voice into indifference.

'I need to get to work. Was there something you particularly wanted to discuss with me other than the contents of this morning's paper?'

'Actually there is something I wanted to discuss with you,' he said.

'Yes?' Her tone was abrupt.

He made her wait for his reply.

'I have a solution to our little problem.'

'What sort of solution?'

Again he let the silence continue unbearably.

'The sort of solution that will dispel all the rumours and restore family faith in the two miscreants.'

'A miracle?' she said with a rueful edge to her voice.

She heard him chuckle.

'Not quite a miracle but an amazing occurrence for all that.'

'What?'

'Marriage.'

'Marriage?' She almost choked on the word, 'Whose marriage?'

There was an infinitesimal pause.

'Our marriage.'

This time it was her who let the silence continue.

'I think we should get married as soon as possible,' he said evenly.

'I think you need to see a psychiatrist,' she shot back. 'I'm not marrying you!'

'Never say never, sweetheart.' He gave another little chuckle.

Jasmine felt as if someone had just walked over her grave. A cold shudder of fear ran through her and her fingers on the telephone grew white-knuckled in panic.

'My parents would never allow such a thing to happen,' she said with as much confidence as she could muster.

'Are you sure?'

'Of course I'm sure! My father would rather die than allow me to marry you.'

'You don't know your father very well then.'

'What do you mean by that?' A flicker of consternation settled in her chest, causing her breathing to trip and become erratic.

'I just spoke to him a few minutes ago.'

'And?'

'And he suggested we should get married as soon as possible.'

CHAPTER TWO

JASMINE felt as if she were going to faint.

The room tilted before her eyes and she had to grasp the edge of the telephone table to anchor her shaking body.

'You can't possibly mean to carry it out,' she managed to croak. 'I mean—it's unthinkable! We're strangers!'

'I don't know about that,' he countered. 'We're almost related now that your sister is married to my stepbrother. Besides, we've spent the night together; I'd say that covers a lot of ground.'

'Not the sort of ground I like to be on!' she shot back. 'I'm not marrying anyone and, even if I was, you'd be the very last person on my list.'

'Flattered, I'm sure,' he drawled insolently.

'I mean it, Connor,' she insisted. 'Marriage is an outdated institution constructed by men to gain control over women.'

'I'm sure your sisters would be very disappointed to hear your views considering that each of them have found and secured themselves a husband within the last year.'

'More fool them.'

He laughed. 'Come on, Jasmine. I promise to be a good husband.'

'You don't know the meaning of the word.'

'Which one? Good or husband?'

'Both.'

'It will have to be a quiet ceremony, of course,' he said.

'I'm not marrying you!'

'And I don't know if your parents will want you to wear white.'

'I'm not mar—'

'And I don't think we need bother with a long honeymoon.'

19

'I'm not going to—'

'But then again, it could be fun.'

She slammed the phone down in frustration. How dare he mock her?

The telephone pealed and she picked it up and thrust her finger on the answer button immediately.

'Go to hell, Connor Harrowsmith!'

She left the phone off the hook and wandered about her tiny apartment in agitation. She was already forty minutes late for the clinic. A few more wasn't going to make or break anything.

She had to sort out this misunderstanding, but how? Perhaps she could call her parents and explain.

She picked up the receiver and quickly dialled the number. Her father answered in his usual Eucharistic tones.

'Good morning. Bishop Byrne speaking.'

'Father, it's me.'

'Jasmine.' She heard him suck in a breath. 'I wondered when you'd get around to calling.'

'I wanted to explain—'

'Your mother is in a state,' he cut across her. 'I've had to call Dr Pullenby. It's been in every paper.'

'It's not my fault. You see it was—'

'Don't tell me the Devil made you do it.' His tone was impatient. 'Do you know how many times I hear that in a week? Do you?'

'Connor and I hardly know—'

'At least he's offered to do the decent thing.'

'Decent?' Jasmine was incredulous. Connor Harrowsmith didn't know the meaning of the word.

'But I'm not performing the ceremony,' he said. 'It would go against everything I believe in.'

'I'm not marrying him.'

'Yes you are,' her father said. 'Or you'll never see either your mother or me again.'

Jasmine couldn't believe her ears. Surely her parents' moral code wasn't more important than their own flesh and blood?

'I understand,' she answered in a detached tone.

'You'd better, young lady,' her father added. 'You've caused quite enough trouble as it is. I've had to negotiate my way through a conversation with the Archbishop this morning. I assured him that you and Finn's brother will be getting married within a month at the very latest.'

'A month!'

'I'd be happier if it were next week. For all we know you could already be carrying his child.'

Jasmine reared away from the telephone in shock.

'He's not the sort of husband I would've liked for you, of course, but then you've always been wilful and disobedient. Perhaps having a difficult husband will teach you the lessons you've always refused to learn.'

Jasmine was lost for words.

'I think it's best if you stay away from your mother for a few days at least,' he added. 'She's terribly upset.'

Jasmine knew enough about her parents to know both of them were upset and used each other's reactions as excuses not to see her. Her father's insistence over her mother's reluctance could be read as his own and, while it pained her, she knew from experience there was little she could do about it. Once their minds were made up they were set in stone; there was simply nothing she could say or do to change them.

She went to work with steps that dragged. Never had she felt less like facing the problems of others. Her own were banking up behind her, threatening to overwhelm her.

She sat listening with one ear to the lament of yet another recovering addict who had some sort of axe to grind over why he wasn't receiving the sort of support he wanted, all the time wondering to herself who was going to support her over this new obstacle.

Todd, the other counsellor, tossed the morning paper on the desk in front of her at lunch time.

'I didn't know we had someone famous working amongst us,' he said with a grin.

Jasmine gave him a twisted half-smile and opened the paper.

She was on page ten.

It wasn't a particularly flattering photo. One of the shoe-string straps of her dress had slipped, revealing a little more of her upper cleavage than was commonly seen in the Montford parish.

She looked furtive and guilty.

She slammed the paper shut and scowled.

'I'll kill him.'

'Who?' Todd asked. 'The photographer?'

'No.' She spun herself out of the office chair. 'The man I slept with.'

Todd's eyebrows rose.

'It's not what you think.' She turned back to look at him.

'I'm not thinking anything.' Todd held up his hands in a gesture of innocence.

'I hate him to hell and back.'

'Strong words from a bishop's daughter.'

'I'm being disowned because of that jerk!'

'Maybe he's done you a favour.' Todd's expression was wry.

She turned away and shuffled the papers on her desk.

'I think I'll take some time off,' she said. 'I need to get away until the dust settles.'

'That's fine. I'll keep an eye on your clients for you.'

'Thanks, Todd.' She gave him a grateful half-smile. 'I really appreciate it.'

The New South Wales south coast had been a bolt-hole for Jasmine for as long as she could remember. For years she'd been driving out of the noise and activity of Sydney to the solitude of long, lonely beaches where her footprints in the sand were the only ones left there all day. She found the roar of the waves therapeutic, calming the inner tension she nearly always felt when surrounded by her family.

One of her mother's friends allowed her to use their little holiday house on their block, a short walk from Pelican Head. It wasn't flash, but it was safe and secure and without a telephone so no one could find her. Lately she'd found she needed more and more time alone; solitude was becoming as addictive as some of the substances her clients at the clinic were in the clutches of. It was only when she was alone she felt safe from her family's disapproval. She saw it in their eyes whenever they focused on her: Jezebel, temptress, sinner.

The trouble was, no one could understand.

No one could possibly understand.

She put her few things in the beach house and, hiding the key in its usual place under a log near the tallest of the three gum trees, made her way to the beach.

The autumn wind had picked up, stirring the waves into frenzy as they lashed at the shore. Jasmine tied her long hair back with a hair-tie and faced the wind full on, closing her eyes and breathing in the salt and spray like a restorative drug.

She sighed with pleasure and began walking, her feet sinking in the water-soaked sand. She trudged on, determined to walk off the image of Connor Harrowsmith's sardonic face.

She still couldn't believe she'd mistakenly gone into his room, especially as she hadn't really wanted to stay in the hotel in the first place. Sam had insisted, saying she didn't want her wedding day memories spoilt with the news of someone being killed on the way home through drink-driving. Well, her wedding memories were probably going to be spoilt anyway once she heard about the press release involving her sister and the best man.

The best man! Huh! He was the worst man. Just the sort of man she avoided at all costs—too handsome and too rich to be responsible for his reckless actions. He drove fast cars and gallivanted around the world's hot spots, all the time in search of the ultimate experience.

Finn had laughingly described some of his stepbrother's exploits—affairs with actresses, married women some of them, and of course his propensity to gamble. Her eyes had widened at the amount Finn had said Connor had won in Las Vegas. She hadn't thought people ever won that amount of money but it seemed Connor had and had used it to set himself up in some sort of computer business. From all accounts his business was expanding exponentially and he had branches in each Australian capital city and was now looking abroad.

Damn him! She skirted around a heap of twisted kelp and willed herself to stop thinking about him.

Marriage! Huh! As if he were any sort of husband a woman might want!

She kicked a piece of sponge with one foot and watched as the wind took over its journey, rolling it over and over until the raging water swallowed it whole.

She turned to go back the way she'd come and pulled up short when she noticed a tall figure coming in her direction.

She tensed; there was something very familiar about that long, easy gait. She blinked the grains of sand out of her eyes and peered a little harder. As he drew closer Jasmine knew there was only one man with that taunting smile.

She considered making a run for it but the sand beneath her feet was heavy with the wash from the high tide and she knew she'd stumble and twist an ankle before she covered any great distance. There was nothing else to do other than face him and ask him what the hell he thought he was doing here.

She waited until he was less than three strides away.

'What the hell do you think you're doing?' She had to almost shout the words over the roar of the surf.

'I'm beachcombing,' he said, holding up a rather nice shell for her inspection.

She slapped his hand away and stomped past him to head back.

'Go away! I don't want to see you.'

He fell into step beside her, his long legs making short work of the heavy sand.

'But I want to see you.'

'Why?' She spun to face him, her hair blowing into her mouth. She brushed it aside angrily and glared up at him. 'You're wasting your time. I have nothing to say to you other than get lost.'

'But I have something to say to you.'

'I don't want to hear it.'

'But it might be the most important news,' he pointed out. 'Something so significant that perhaps years later when you walk along this beach with your grandkids your mind will wander and you'll find yourself thinking, Now, what was it that nice young man had to say? You'll rebuke yourself for not having heard him out.'

'Don't be so ridiculous!' She began stomping through the sand once more. 'You're not a nice person and I don't care what you have to say. I've never cared and I never will!'

'I think you do care, Jasmine, but you choose to hide that from most people behind that gruff I-don't-give-a-damn façade you're always wearing.'

Jasmine didn't let him see how close to the mark his assessment came. She lifted her chin in the air and kept walking, determined to shake him off one way or the other.

'That's a nice place where you're staying,' he said after a stormy silence broken only by the sucking sound of the sand around their feet.

She stopped in her tracks and shot him an accusatory glance.

'How did you know where to find me?'

His dark eyes gleamed. 'Now wouldn't you like to know?'

'I would, actually.' Her tone was arctic. 'Did you have me followed?'

His expression gave nothing away and her frown deepened.

'Don't panic.' He smiled down at her. 'I won't tell anyone your little secret.'

She tore her eyes away from the glint of mockery shining in his. Fear churned in the cavity of her stomach at the thought of her haven being discovered by someone so invading as Connor Harrowsmith. She'd never be able to come here again without thinking about him; her private paradise was now occupied by the very Devil himself.

'You really shouldn't disappear without telling someone where you're going,' he said when still she didn't speak. 'It's not safe.'

'It was safe until five minutes ago,' she bit out.

'It's still safe.' His eyes had softened along with his voice. 'Now I'm here to protect you.'

'I don't need you to protect me.'

'I think you will be very glad of my protection when I tell you what's in the afternoon paper.'

She felt her breathing snag somewhere in the middle of her chest. Clenching her hands into fists she forced herself to meet his dark chocolate-brown gaze.

'What do you mean?'

The line of his mouth was grim. 'An interview with Roy Holden's wife.'

'Oh, my God!' She sucked in a shaky breath, her face blanching in shock.

'No doubt the lure of money for the interview put any of her previous scruples to rest.'

Jasmine's voice was hollow and emotionless when she finally found it. 'I can't see what this has to do with you.'

'It has everything to do with me,' he argued. 'You're now my fiancée.'

'I am nothing of the sort!'

His dark brows arched at the vehemence of her denial.

'Honey—' she felt herself shiver at his casually delivered endearment '—if you don't marry me within a month you'll find yourself without a family. Your father is serious; he's determined to denounce you. Harsh I know, but then he's on high moral ground.'

She stared at him. It was strange hearing him use the very words she'd used—was it only two days ago?—when thinking of her father's moral code?

'But you can't seriously want to marry me,' she said.

He gave a little shrug. 'I've got nothing else better to do.'

'Thanks.'

She spun back to face the climb up to the cliff path, her back stiff with pride. She felt him behind her with every clawing hold she took and wished she hadn't been so hasty. She could just imagine him tucked in behind her, grinning to himself at the uninterrupted view of her bottom as she scaled the track.

Damn him!

She lost her hold and slipped backwards, taking an uprooted plant with her.

'Hey.' He caught her between his legs, clamping his thighs to secure her. 'Watch your step. This path is lethal if you're not concentrating.'

She wasn't brave enough to look upwards. She'd already seen a glimpse of what was packaged between those strong thighs and she didn't want to remind herself of it.

She scrambled forward out of the vice of his legs and, with as much grace as she could gather, made her way to the top, her breathing hard and fast.

He joined her on the path, his own breathing steady and even.

'You need to get fit,' he said. 'Then you wouldn't be quite so puffed out.'

'I'm not puffed out!' she puffed. 'I'm angry.'

He grinned at her. 'I know of a very good exercise.'

'Shut up!' She clamped her hands over her ears. 'I don't want to hear about it.'

His hands covered hers and pulled them away from her

head. She wanted to tear them from his loose grasp but the drop behind her forestalled her.

'Jasmine, listen to me.'

She closed her eyes to shut him out.

'Go away. I don't even want to look at you.'

She heard him sigh but didn't open her eyes. Surely he'd just go away as long as she kept giving him the brush off. Most men would have left hours ago.

'You're a stubborn little thing, aren't you?' he observed.

'Say what you like,' she threw back at him. 'I'm not listening to you.'

'There's a whole lot I could say but now is perhaps not the right time. We seem to have company.'

Jasmine's eyes sprang open and she glanced past him to see who else was going to spoil her sanctuary.

'There's no one there.' She met his dark gaze once more.

'I beg to differ.' His hands tightened on hers a fraction as he inclined his head to the left of where she was standing.

She looked down and shrieked at the coiled brown snake no more than a metre and a half from her feet. She flung herself forward into Connor's arms, uncaring that he was the enemy and could probably do her more harm in the long run. She decided to take her chances; snakes were not her favourite creature.

Connor held her against him as he began backing slowly away from the snake's uncoiling form.

'It's OK.' His tone was enviably calm. 'He's not all that interested in us. I saw a couple of geckoes on my way down so that's probably why he's here.'

'I hate snakes.' She gave a little shudder.

She felt his laugh rumble against her cheek where she was pressed so tightly against his chest.

'I wouldn't have one as a pet either.'

He loosened his hold as they came to the end of the path well away from the snake.

'There, what did I tell you—safe and sound.'

She looked around, inspecting the rocky ground for snake trails, but it was all clear.

'Thank you.' It was the least she could say under the circumstances.

They both knew the drop behind her had been there and that one startled step backwards would have sent her over. She felt a funny sensation in the pit of her stomach that he of all people had come to her rescue.

'No problem,' he said, his tone light and unaffected by the recent presence of imminent danger. 'Snakes I can handle. Threatening fathers are another thing entirely.'

The wryness of his tone reminded her of his own family battles. She didn't really know all that much about the Harrowsmith family except what Sam had let slip once or twice. She knew Connor's mother had died not long after her marriage to Julian Harrowsmith, leaving Connor at the age of four under his guardianship. Connor's own father was unknown; apparently he was the consequence of a passionate affair his mother had while still in her teens. Finn, the child of Julian and his second wife Harriet, spoke of his stepbrother with affection, although she sensed they were not all that close.

'How has your family reacted to this latest scandal of yours?' she asked as they began to walk along the bush track to the road.

His expression was guarded. 'They've made the usual noises about disinheriting me and so on.'

'That's terrible! You should do something!'

'I don't have a lot of choice just now,' he answered. 'The sooner this thing settles down the better. I have some big financial commitments pending with my overseas interests and I don't want to let the money from my mother's estate be redirected.'

'Could your stepfather really do that?' She stopped to look up at him, her brow furrowed in concern.

'He's one of Sydney's leading lawyers.' His eyes hardened momentarily. 'He can do anything.'

She bit her lip and kept walking.

'But surely you have enough money of your own by now to call his bluff?'

Connor's hand on her arm stopped her. He turned her to face him, the silence of the bush enveloping them in a type of intimacy she'd never felt with anyone before. It unsettled her, making her feel as if he stepped past some sort of barrier she had carefully constructed around herself all her life.

'I have plenty of money, yes, but I can't access my mother's until I marry,' he answered.

'What?'

'It was the way the will was written. I suppose my mother didn't want some poor girl to go through what she had as a teenage single mother. She wasn't taking any chances, even if I were her son and only an infant at the time of writing her will.'

Jasmine gnawed at her lip once more.

'Marriage is such a big step.' She looked at the open neck of his shirt instead of into his dark eyes. 'I wish I could help you but...'

'What will you do about your family?' he asked.

'I can handle them.'

'And the Holden interview? Can you handle that?'

Her gaze was worried when it returned to his. 'I have been through all this before, you know.'

'Yes.' His half-smile was wry. 'You certainly know how to rock the religious boat, don't you?'

She found herself smiling reluctantly at his choice of words.

'It wasn't intentional, I assure you.'

'All the same, this recent calamity won't help your father's chances of promotion. Finn has indicated that Elias has set his sights on being the next Archbishop when the present one retires.'

Jasmine had heard it too and it only added to her worries.

She knew her father was grasping at Connor's marriage solution with thoughts of his own salvation in mind, not hers.

'Marriage has never been a particular goal of mine,' she said. 'I can't see myself chained to a kitchen sink for the next fifty years.'

'Not all marriages are like that.'

'Aren't they?'

His hand disturbed the thicket of his dark, windswept hair, giving him an even wilder out of control look. His jaw was heavily shadowed as if he hadn't shaved since the day of her sister's wedding. She wondered what it would feel like to have him kiss her now with his lean jaw all scratchy and intensely, disturbingly male.

She gave a little shiver and tore her eyes away from his face.

'Are you cold?' he asked.

'No.'

They walked on a bit further in silence.

Connor watched her covertly as she walked beside him, the sweet fragrance of her hair reaching his nostrils from time to time as the wind lifted the chestnut strands across her face.

He felt that familiar gut-tightening reaction he'd experienced the very first time he'd met her. She was so unlike all the women he'd known, and he was the first to admit he'd known rather too many of late. It was time to settle down after that last disastrous affair with the Texan heiress—he had to take stock and get his priorities sorted once and for all. He owed that to his mother's memory if nothing else.

He couldn't help thinking his mother would have approved of the defiant figure beside him. Jasmine was like a breath of fresh sea air with her spirited defiance and spitfire tongue, but he was almost certain that underneath that prickly exterior she was already starting to melt. He saw it in her grey-blue eyes when she thought he wasn't looking. There was a hunger there and he fully intended to satiate it...

Jasmine listened to the crunch of leaves and twigs under

their feet and the warble of the magpies in the gum trees overhead. The sound of cicadas filled the air; it was as if they knew the long, hot summer was over and the shortening days would silence their chorus soon.

'How long are you planning to stay here?' he asked after a few more minutes.

'A day or two,' she answered, not comfortable with revealing all her movements to him.

'I left my car up at the beach house,' he informed her.

'How did you find it?'

'I just drove up the driveway and there it was.'

She gave him a reproving look.

'I mean, how did you know I was here? It's not exactly on the beaten track.'

'Well, it's rather a long story but I was discussing real estate with someone and they mentioned a property down here they thought I might be interested in, and I bought it.'

Jasmine forced her feet to keep moving forward, hoping her voice sounded suitably uninterested. 'Oh, really?'

'You probably know it quite intimately,' he said. 'It's not all that far from you.'

She stopped so suddenly she almost stumbled over her own feet.

'Which place?'

His dark eyes glinted down at her.

'The old house down the road.'

She knew it well. She generally avoided it because it appeared deserted and dilapidated, sad almost, as if whoever had lived there had not been all that happy with life. The fact that Connor had bought it seemed to her to be a deliberate act on his part to force his presence on both her and the neglected property.

She wasn't sure which she was defending when she turned on him. 'You have no right to come here!'

'I beg to differ as I have every right in the world. The place is now mine, so I can come and go as I please.'

She gave him a venomous glare.

'You're doing this deliberately, aren't you? You're invading every area of my life to get your own way.'

'Don't be so prickly,' he chided. 'Nothing was further from my mind.'

'Don't lie to me!' She almost shouted the words. 'If you think this will make me marry you to get you out of trouble, forget it. There's nothing on this planet that would induce me to become your wife—nothing!'

He let her vent her spleen, standing quietly and calmly, which only served to infuriate her even more.

She turned abruptly and stomped away, her head down in case he caught a glimpse of her stinging tears of anger.

Somehow she lost him at the turn-off. She took the long way back to the house that few people knew and, when she was sure he wasn't following, sat by the creek bed and howled out her frustration, leaving it another hour before she finally returned to the little beach house.

When she got there Connor's car was gone. But when she looked down at the dusty gravel of the driveway she could see where his tyres had been and it made her feel uneasy.

He'd be back, she was sure; that much about him she did know.

He'd be back.

Jasmine decided after another hour of sickening dread, that Connor would reappear and find her still crying, that her best course of action would be to leave.

She packed with none of her usual attention to detail, thrusting things untidily into the back of her car as if the hounds of hell were on her tail.

She gave the beach house a cursory swipe with a dust cloth and mop and hightailed it out of the driveway before she changed her mind.

Thankfully there was hardly any traffic on the roads and

although she had to stop once for petrol the trip back to her inner city flat was uneventful.

Her flat seemed poky and stuffy after the fresh air of Pelican Head. She felt claustrophobic and cornered, as if her days were numbered like someone on death row.

Ever since Connor Harrowsmith had come into her life she'd felt unsafe. He made her feel things she didn't want to feel. He made her so angry she wanted to hit him. She wanted to tear at his mocking eyes and stop him laughing at her from behind those chocolate irises.

The telephone buzzed beside her as she sat on her bed.

She looked at it indecisively for five more rings before snatching up the receiver.

'Jasmine?' Her mother's voice was wobbly—probably from a recent bout of tears.

'Hello, Mum.'

'Jasmine, you have to marry him. Please, darling, if for no other reason, do it for me.'

Jasmine felt fresh tears at the back of her own eyes and she swallowed deeply.

'Mum, I—'

'The parish council has called a meeting. They're thinking of withdrawing their support for your father.' Her mother's voice cracked. 'And with the synod meeting in a matter of weeks, you know how this will impact on his plans for the position of Archbishop.'

'Mum—'

'Jasmine, I've done all I can but this is the last straw. I can't see your father ruined. The last time was bad enough and now we have to relive it all again, splashed all over the press.'

'That's not my fault.'

'It is all your fault!' her mother screeched.

Jasmine's hand around the telephone tightened as she fought to control her temper. It was so unfair! Was there no one on this earth who would suspend judgement long enough to find out all the details first?

'Your father has decided on an ultimatum,' her mother continued.

'Which is?'

'He doesn't wish to see you again unless you agree to marry Connor immediately.'

'What about you?' Jasmine asked pointedly. 'Will you see me again if I don't?'

There was a telling silence at the end of the line.

'Darling—' her mother paused for breath '—you know how difficult this is for me but your father and I agree—'

Jasmine had heard enough; she knew she was cornered and there was no point fighting any more. Whenever her mother used that tone of voice she felt guilty. It was like an intolerable load on her back to hear that defeated, long-suffering tone. She loved her mother and, deep down, knew she would do anything to relieve her suffering, even if it cost her dearly.

'All right,' she said after another tight silence. 'I'll do it.'

Her mother's gushing relief should have encouraged her but it didn't. Instead it made her realise she had just stepped into a noose that had been laid out especially for her.

And at the other end of the rope was Connor Harrowsmith, who would no doubt be smiling in victory at her final capitulation.

CHAPTER THREE

JASMINE had no way of contacting Connor but he must have known she'd changed her mind for when she got back home from the clinic the following day he was waiting for her outside her flat.

He was leaning up against his shiny black Maserati, this time dressed a little more formally in a business shirt, tie and black trousers which seemed to make his long legs look even longer.

His eyes meshed with hers as she came across the road from the bus stop.

'Hello.'

She found it hard to hold his look and inspected the cracked pavement at her feet.

'What brings you here?'

'What do you think?' he asked.

She gave a non-committal shrug before chancing a look at his handsome face.

'I don't suppose you've brought an engagement ring with you?' She hoped her tone sounded flippant enough to cover the trepidation she was currently feeling.

'I did, as a matter of fact,' he said, surprising her completely.

'Oh.' What else could she say?

'It was my grandmother's so I hope it fits. If it doesn't, we'll have it adjusted.' He slipped his hand into the top pocket of his shirt and handed her a little velvet box, the edges worn with age.

She took it from him, trying not to touch his fingers as she did so. She opened the box and for a long moment looked at the ruby surrounded by tiny diamonds.

'Go on, try it on.'

She took it out and slipped it on to her finger, somehow not at all surprised to find it was a perfect fit.

She lifted her troubled gaze to his. 'It's beautiful. It must be very valuable.'

'It is.'

She didn't know what to say. It seemed like sacrilege to be wearing such a ring for all the wrong reasons. It wasn't a proper engagement in any sense of the word, nor would it ever be a proper marriage.

'Would you like a drink or something?' She hunted for her keys in her bag, trying to cover her unease with forced politeness.

'Sure.'

He followed her up the pathway to the old terrace house where she occupied the top floor. She hoped he wasn't noticing the cracked and peeling paint on the stairwell as they went up. She imagined he lived in some sort of playboy mansion in an exclusive suburb and was probably turning his aristocratic nose up with distaste with each and every step he took behind her.

'This is cosy,' he said, surprising her again as he followed her into her tiny flat.

She tossed down her keys without answering.

'Have you lived here long?'

'A few months,' she answered. 'It's close to the clinic.'

'Ah, the clinic.' There was something in his tone that unsettled her. 'I've heard all about the clinic.'

'From whom?' Her words were sharpened by her anger at her parents' ultimatum. She could just imagine them describing the run-down building to him, lamenting the fact that their church school educated daughter had chosen such a career path, and an underpaid one at that.

'Not from anyone you'd know,' he said.

'My parents haven't talked to you about it?' She eyeballed him directly.

'I'm afraid my conversations with your parents so far have concentrated on other topics.'

She could just imagine!

'You weren't too put off by one of my father's interminable lectures about right and wrong?'

'Your father and I have come to an impasse. He thinks he's right and I think he's wrong.'

'About what?'

'About you.'

'Me?' She stared at him.

'Yes, you. He doesn't know you at all, does he?'

Jasmine couldn't help feeling a little bit overexposed. How had he come to that conclusion? He hardly knew her! Surely that one night in his bed, innocent as it was, couldn't have given him any sort of insight into her character?

'I'm not sure I know what you mean,' she hedged.

'Do you know, to an outsider you seem to be rather a misfit in your family,' he said, watching her intently.

She turned away from his all-seeing eyes to switch on a lamp. Her tiny flat didn't get much afternoon sun and the subdued lighting gave the room an intimate atmosphere she felt uncomfortable sharing with him.

'What makes you think that?' she asked off-handedly.

She watched him out of the corner of her eye as he sat down on her second-hand sofa chair, the one with the springs showing through the cushions, noticing he didn't even flinch as he sat on their protruding coils.

'Your hair for one thing.'

'My hair?' She touched the cascading strands around her face self-consciously; no matter what she did, her hair would just not stay up.

'Your sisters all have straight blonde hair; your hair is chestnut and curly.'

'So?'

'Your parents are both fair.'

'Perhaps I'm a throw-back.' She met his eyes across the room. 'It happens from time to time.'

His dark gaze held hers.

She felt increasingly uncomfortable under his scrutiny, frightened in case he would eventually see through the wall of indifference she'd erected around herself for protection.

'What would you like to drink?' she asked, desperate for a subject change even if it meant extending his visit, loath as she was to do it.

'What will you have?' he asked.

'I'm not a drinker,' she said without apology. 'So I've only juice, tea or coffee or water. The coffee's instant by the way.'

'Water's fine,' he said, surprising her yet again. 'It's been quite warm today, hasn't it?'

She wasn't so sure about the day but she was feeling increasingly warm with his dark eyes on her all the time!

'I didn't go outside much,' she answered. 'I was tied up with a workshop all day.' She went through to the kitchen and got two glasses out of the cupboard above the sink.

'What do you do at the clinic?' he asked from behind her.

She waited until she'd filled both glasses before turning to answer him. He took the glass she held out to him, his fingers brushing hers.

'I'm involved with the rehab team.' She cradled her own glass with both hands. 'We teach the patients life skills, help them find employment—that sort of thing.'

'Rewarding work.'

She gave him a rueful look.

'Sometimes.' She took a sip of water. 'But I'm afraid there aren't as many happy endings as I'd like.'

'People have free will. You can't always make them change unless they want it for themselves.'

'I know.' She put the glass down on the sink. 'But I have to try.'

'Because of your family background?' he asked.

She looked at him when he said that.

It amazed her later to think how close she had been to admitting to him how right he was, but something had stopped her. She didn't want him to have access to any part of her private life; it was less hurtful that way.

She pushed herself away from the sink and made to move past him.

'If you've finished your water I think you should be going. I have some calls to make.'

His hand came down on her arm and held her fast. She forced herself to meet his gaze but it took every ounce of her pride to hold it without blinking.

'I haven't finished talking to you,' he said. 'We have a wedding to plan.'

'Plan it without me.' Her tone was dismissive as if they were discussing a picnic she hadn't yet made her mind up to attend. 'I'm not fussy.'

'So it seems.' His tone was dry. 'But, all the same, I'd like your input.'

'I don't want a big wedding,' she insisted. 'A registry office will do and no guests.'

'What about photographs?'

'No photographs.'

'You might regret that one day when the kids ask to see them.'

She wrenched her arm out of his hold and glared up at him. 'What kids?'

She didn't care for the dark glitter that had suddenly come into his eyes. 'Ours, of course.'

She felt a flicker of heat pool traitorously in her belly at the thought of being swollen with his child but as quickly as she could she stamped it out.

'If you think this marriage will ever be consummated you're very much mistaken.'

He quirked one aristocratic brow.

'Never say never, sweetheart.' The corner of his mouth

twisted mockingly. 'Such emphatic statements have a nasty habit of coming back dressed up as humble pie.'

'I don't want to marry you in the first place!' she fumed. 'If I have to sleep with you it will make it a hundred times worse!'

'How so?'

'You know how so.' She clenched her fists in agitation.

'I'll be gentle—'

'Oh, for God's sake!' She wanted to stamp her foot over his toes in frustration. 'Stop making fun of me!'

'I'm not making fun of you; I'm simply informing you of my intentions.'

'Your intentions are to milk this situation for all it's worth. I know what you're up to. This is about getting back at your stepfather, isn't it?'

His eyes narrowed slightly and she continued heatedly. 'I'm known as a notorious tart; everyone knows it and, even if they'd forgotten, they were reminded of it in the papers two days in a row. What better way to rub your family's nose in it than to marry me to spite them?'

'If you'll remember, the notion of marrying you was your father's suggestion,' he pointed out in even tones.

She'd forgotten that little detail but it made no difference.

'Either way it's still his penance for you. It's all the same thing, isn't it? I've been cast as the devil's gateway in all this; it's irrelevant who's actually oiled the hinges.'

His chuckle of amusement broke the tension.

'What's so funny?' She frowned at him darkly, trying to suppress the twitch of her mouth that had been precipitated by his.

'You are.'

'I'm not trying to be funny.' She scowled.

'I know, and that's why you're so successful at making me laugh.' He touched her gently on the cheek. 'Not many people can make me laugh; not many people at all.'

Jasmine couldn't quite get rid of the feeling that something other than mutual amusement was being passed between them. It was more subtle than that; like a delicate, slender thread had passed across the room, linking them in an indefinable way.

Her cheek still tingled from his butterfly-like touch, her senses now on full alert at his nearness. He was half a step away from her. She could even feel the heat coming off his body as he stood looking down at her, his firm mouth relaxed in a small sexy smile that sent a silent message straight to her feminine core.

He closed the distance without appearing to have moved at all. For a fleeting moment she wondered if in fact it had been her who had shifted in response to a subconscious desire to feel his mouth on hers.

He bent his head as if in slow motion.

The anticipation was like torture to Jasmine's already throbbing lips, her snagging breath escaping in sharp, painful little intervals from between them. As his head came closer and closer her lips opened automatically as if commanded to do so by the flash of desire in his eyes.

His lips touched hers in a tentative 'hardly there' kiss that made her lips buzz with sensation even more. He did it again, and again, each time the pressure increasing a mere fraction as if he were tasting her for the very first time.

She'd had enough.

She wanted him to kiss her, really kiss her.

She grasped his dark head between her hands and took over the kiss with all the pent-up passion she'd been feeling from the first moment his eyes had met hers in the church at her sister's wedding. Her tongue found his and he tightened his hold around her waist, pulling her into his hard frame, leaving her in absolutely no doubt of his body's instant reaction.

He wanted her.

For whatever reason, he wanted her and knowing it made her own response to him fire out of control. Her mouth became frenzied on his, kissing him greedily as if he were the very air she needed to breathe to keep alive.

He returned the frantic pleas of her mouth with commandeering ones of his own, his tongue leaving no corner of her mouth unexplored, staked and claimed.

She felt as if she belonged to him now.

He'd branded her with an invisible brand that left her useless without his touch on her fevered skin.

She craved it.

She craved it like the thirsty crave water or the hungry hunger for food. Every cell in her body was rising up to greet him, every nerve leaping just under her skin to feel the pressure of his fingers running over her, caressing her. Her breasts felt heavy, their pointed buds tight against the cotton of her bra, straining, aching to get closer to him.

She felt the rasp of his evening shadow as he moved his mouth slightly, sending a sharp burst of sensation to the pit of her stomach. Never had she been more aware of his masculinity. Her heightened awareness fuelled the leaping flames of her desire into a conflagration; she was completely at his mercy, wanting him even more than her pride, which until now had been so important to her.

As if he sensed her surrender, his kiss changed to a seductive caress, his lips leaving hers to move down to the sensitive skin of her neck. She felt the warm brush of his fingers undoing the top three buttons of her simple white blouse, the fabric folding open to give him access to the creamy shadow of her breasts lying waiting, aching for his touch.

He gave her an opened mouth kiss on the upper side of her right breast; the heat of his mouth firing her senses to an intolerable level. He did the same to the other and she thought she would scream if he didn't finish the job properly by uncovering her breasts completely.

His hand came up to gently cup her cheek, lifting her face so she had no choice but to look up at him.

'You know I could do right now what most men would do

in this situation, yet something tells me it's not the right time.' His voice was deep and husky. 'But I promise you I will finish this. You have my word.'

Jasmine found the sparkle of unrelieved desire in his eyes compelling; she couldn't look away if she tried. She swallowed the restriction in her throat; her intake of breath catching in tiny little tugs all the way down into her lungs.

He released his hold and stepped away from her.

'I have to go now,' he said. 'Will you be all right?'

Pride came to her rescue. What did he think she was, some sort of sexual desperado?

'I think I'll just about manage,' she said tightly.

He smiled and touched her on the cheek once more.

'Till next time.'

She didn't answer him.

She didn't trust herself not to beg him to come back and finish what he'd started right here and now.

She watched as he walked from the room and then listened to his footsteps as he traversed the tiny hall, heard the door open and registered the click of the lock as it closed behind him, still without moving a millimetre from where he'd left her.

She was frozen to the spot by the sudden realisation that her hatred of him had vaporised, leaving in its place a much more destructive emotion. The sort of emotion she didn't want to feel for any man, the sort of emotion that would spell disaster for someone such as her.

She didn't want to love him.

Damn him!

She wasn't going to give in!

Jasmine did all she could to avoid Connor's calls.

She left the phone off the hook for hours and didn't answer the door if the doorbell rang. She worked the most unfriendly hours she could, repeatedly taking the graveyard shift to avoid facing him until she was ready.

She wasn't ready.

She wondered if she'd ever be ready.

She only had to think of him and her stomach would cave in, the sweet hollow feeling reminding her of an aching physical need of him.

As if summoned by her thoughts, he materialised just as she was leaving the clinic at midnight the following Friday. He was standing outside, leaning against his car, his dark, hooded gaze fixed on her.

He pushed himself away from the car and before she could say anything picked up her left hand and inspected it. He dropped it and asked, 'Where's your ring?'

She found the abruptness of his tone intensely irritating.

'I don't wear it in public.'

'Why not?' He almost barked the words at her.

Her eyebrows rose and she swung away from him to make her way to the bus stop. She hadn't taken three steps before he'd caught the tail of her untucked shirt and pulled her back.

'Hey!' She slapped at his hand. 'This is my best shirt!'

'It's too big for you and it's the wrong colour,' he said.

She felt herself bristle at his criticism.

'I like it.' She snatched the fabric out of his grasp and dusted herself off exaggeratedly.

'Why haven't you answered my calls?' he asked.

'I've been busy.'

'You've been avoiding me.'

'No I haven't,' she lied.

'Why don't you wear my ring?'

'I thought it was my ring?' she shot back.

'Don't split hairs.'

'It's too expensive.'

'Oh, for God's sweet sake, Jasmine, it's an engagement ring. It's supposed to be expensive.'

'I don't like wearing expensive jewellery.'

'Then I'll get you something cheaper.'

'I don't want something cheaper.'

'Then what the hell do you want?' His voice rang out over the deserted street.

'I...' She clamped her mouth shut. She was so close to shouting back that she wanted him—wanted him with every fibre of her being.

'I want to go home,' she said instead. 'It's been a long day.'

He sighed and, taking her arm, led her towards his car. 'It's been a long week,' he said, opening the door for her. 'And it's not over yet.'

She didn't respond. She slipped into the seat with uncharacteristic meekness and silently buckled her seatbelt. She watched as he came round to the driver's side and took his own seat, his glance wrathful as it came her way.

'Don't ever do that again, do you hear me?'

She gave him a frosty look. 'You don't own me.'

'Yet.' He started the car with a violent turn of the key.

She winced at the barely disguised anger simmering under the surface of his one hard-bitten word.

'Did you get out of the wrong side of the bed this morning?' She folded her arms across her chest huffily.

'You could say that.' He recalled the lonely emptiness of his bed that morning, adding with a rueful glance her way, 'It was certainly the wrong bed.'

Her heart sank. Surely he didn't have someone else? A sick feeling came into her stomach, a combination of fear and dashed hopes and mind-blowing jealousy.

'Perhaps you should be a little more careful in your choice of bed partner,' she tossed back.

'I intend to be very careful in future.'

She didn't know what to make of his statement so kept silent.

It was a while before he spoke.

'I suppose you saw the televised interview with Holden's wife on Channel One last night?'

She kept her eyes on her tightly crossed knees.

'No, I didn't.'

She felt his quick glance.

'Why not? Surely you'd want to know what's being said about you.'

She elevated one slim shoulder dismissively. 'What would be the point? It's not as if I can answer my critics.'

'You could give your own interview, tell them your side of the—'

'No!'

She felt his assessing glance once more.

'You sound very determined.'

'I am.'

'The money doesn't tempt you?'

She looked at him at that. 'No, the money doesn't tempt me.'

He turned back to the traffic, his brow creased in a heavy frown.

He knew she didn't know all the facts. How could she? The trouble was, he knew too much. The burden of his knowledge was like a thorn in his side. It niggled at him constantly, but he could hardly blurt out the truth. She would very likely be devastated to hear it so baldly. Better to let her begin to suspect something and then gradually help her to see it...

A wave of protectiveness washed over him, surprising him in its intensity. He wasn't usually the knight in shining armour type; God knew he'd exploited so many relationships in the past any decent white horse would have bucked him off years ago. But there was something about Jasmine that stirred him where no one had stirred him before. He wasn't all that sure he understood it but he knew he had to have her, and her parents' ultimatum was going to make it a whole lot easier than he'd expected.

'I had a call from your father today,' he said after a long pause.

She gave a cynical grunt as he pulled up alongside her terrace house.

'What did he want? A chance to inveigle himself into the registry office proceedings?'

'It seems he's having a rethink about us getting married.' Jasmine tensed.

'Apparently he thinks you could do much better.'

'What did you say?' she asked, not brave enough to look his way.

He gave a deep chuckle that sent shivers up her spine.

'What I told him is not for a bishop's daughter's ears.' He gave her a wry glance. 'Unfortunately, it wasn't all that suitable for a bishop's ears either.'

A bubble of laughter came out of her mouth before she could stop it. She quickly covered it with a self-conscious cough but from the satisfied expression on his face when she looked at him she could tell he'd heard and noted it.

'So the wedding's off?' she asked.

'No, the wedding is not off.'

A funny sensation flickered between her thighs at his emphatic tone.

'Actually, he soon changed his mind again,' he added.

She looked at him warily, wondering what was going on behind that sexy half-smile playing at the corner of his mouth.

'Don't tell me you had to bribe him for my hand?'

He gave a deep rumble of laughter which sent another shiver of sensation right through her.

'Your father is very proud of his organ, isn't he?'

It took her a moment to grasp his meaning but by then it was already too late, her cheeks were fiery red.

'Yes, although it's in some need of repair,' she muttered, trying not to look his way.

'Not enough use?' He threw her a cheeky look.

She didn't answer, but the glance she sent his way spoke for her and he laughed again.

'Once your father cashes the cheque I just donated to the organ fund I don't think we'll hear another word about my unsuitability as a husband.'

'I thought you were short of money.' She frowned at him. 'Isn't that why you need to get married to access your mother's estate?'

His eyes were on the traffic ahead and he waited until someone turning right moved out of his way before he answered.

'I will never be short of money, but the money I want most in the world is what my mother left for me in her will. I guess compared to what I currently earn it may, to some people, seem rather a pittance, but she wanted me to have it and no one, and I mean no one, is going to stop me getting it.'

There was something in his tone that yet again alerted her to some undercurrent of ill-feeling towards his stepparents. She wished she knew more about his childhood, about the grief he must have felt on the death of his mother at such a young age, and his feeling of uncertainty for his future living in a household of people who bore no blood relationship to him. She didn't voice her thoughts, however; she didn't want him to think she had any feelings of any sort where he was concerned, and especially not feelings of empathy.

'You're making a big mistake tying yourself to me,' she warned as he turned the car into the kerb. 'Nothing good can come out of it.'

'Let's wait and see, shall we?' His eyes caught and held hers.

She had to look away; he had an uncanny knack of seeing things she didn't want him to see.

'Thanks for the lift home.' She reached for the door.

He reached across her to open it for her and she instantly shrank back as his muscled arm brushed against her breasts.

He heard her swift intake of breath and, leaning back, gave her a long, studied look.

'Jasmine, answer me one question.'

She turned back to face him. 'What is it?'

He waited a full thirty seconds before he spoke.

'Tell me something.' He paused. 'Are you agreeing to

marry me because of your parents' demands on you or because of my desire to claim my mother's estate?'

What could she say?

Neither?

That she was tempted to marry him just for herself? There was no way she was going to confess that to him! The truth was she did want to marry him. She wasn't entirely sure why. He annoyed her, agitated her, teased her and intrigued her as no one else had ever done but a secret part of her felt drawn to him, as if he alone held the key to her long search for happiness. His laughter stirred her, his touch inflamed her, and his eyes twinkled with passionate promise until she couldn't think straight. But she mustn't let him see the effect he had on her. That must be kept hidden at all costs.

'I've got nothing better to do.' She tossed his previous words back at him casually.

A small smile tugged at his mouth.

'Jasmine Byrne, what the hell am I going to do with you?'

'I don't know.' Her voice came out huskily.

'I know what I want to do.' He closed the distance between them, his arm coming around her shoulder and drawing her close.

She lifted her startled gaze to his descending mouth, her heart tripping in her chest as she felt his warm breath disturb the soft surface of her lips.

'W…what?' She barely breathed the word.

'You know what,' he said and covered her mouth with his.

She didn't want the kiss to end.

She was already mentally rehearsing her invitation for him to come upstairs when he broke the contact and looked down at her with a rueful half-smile.

'I'll call you tomorrow,' he said.

Her fingers reached and fumbled over the door handle and somehow she finally managed to get it open and drag herself from the car without caving in to the temptation to beg.

She stood awkwardly on the pavement, her hands twisted

in front of her just like a gauche schoolgirl coming back from her very first date.

'Go on in,' he said. 'I'll wait until you're safely indoors before I leave.'

She turned on her heels and walked the short distance to the front door, all the time resisting the urge to run back to the car and plead with him to...

'Jasmine?'

His voice stalled her.

She turned back around, faint hope flashing briefly on her features until she saw he was holding something out to her, suspended on the end of his long fingers.

'Your bag,' he said evenly, his expression unreadable.

She walked back to his car with as much dignity as she could and took her bag from him.

'Thank you,' she said stiffly.

He didn't say a word.

She walked back to the front door and after three attempts finally opened it and without a backward glance went inside and closed it behind her.

But even as she stood and listened as his powerful car drove off she was sure she could hear the sound of his mocking laughter filling the night air.

Damn him!

CHAPTER FOUR

THE date for the wedding had been set for the following Friday.

All the way to her parents' house Jasmine's anger had been steadily growing over her father's permission being granted for the mere price of a pipe organ overhaul. She wanted to be angry at Connor for suggesting it, but knew deep down it was her father she was most annoyed with for accepting it.

On her arrival, however, it seemed her mother still had some misgivings.

'Are you sure you know what you're doing?' Frances Byrne asked, her brow furrowed in a frown.

'Of course I know what I'm doing,' she answered, wondering if it were entirely true.

'But darling—' her mother's hands twisted together '—he's so…so…'

'Go on, say it, Frances,' her father cut in impatiently. 'He's a rake and he gambles.'

'And I'm an outrageous tart,' Jasmine shot back. 'A match made in heaven, if you ask me.'

Her father had always found it difficult to deal with her propensity for sarcasm and, as was his custom, shook his head and looked heavenward for guidance.

'Oh, for goodness sake, Elias,' her mother scolded.

'It's all right, Mum,' Jasmine said, sensing a showdown. 'I understand your concern, but this is now between Connor and me.'

Her mother's worried gaze flicked to her husband and back again.

'Jasmine…' She hesitated.

'No, Frances,' her father interrupted her. 'Leave it.'

'But Elias, she has to know some time—'

'If you mean about the organ fund, I already know about that.' She threw her father a caustic glance.

Her father shifted his gaze uncomfortably.

'Elias—' Her mother's voice sounded hollow and her features took on a sickening pallor.

Jasmine's eyes went back and forth between her parents, a sinking feeling coming into her stomach at the lines of tension she could see etched on their faces as they exchanged worried glances.

'What's going on?' she asked.

Her father's lips closed together like a purse being shut.

'Mum?' She turned back to her mother, her frown deepening.

'Nothing's going on,' her mother said, avoiding her eye. 'I'm just being silly, that's all. Too many weddings in one year, I suppose.' She dabbed at her eyes and once she was finished stuffed her handkerchief back up her sleeve, communicating that her brief lapse into sentimentality was now over.

'Jasmine, your mother and I want you to be happy,' her father said in the tone he used for a particularly serious sermon topic. 'But your tendency to rush headlong into things has always been of great concern to us.'

'I'm twenty-four years old,' she said with a touch of bitterness. 'Surely it's time I was left to deal with the consequences of my actions without your intervention.'

Her parents exchanged another nervous, agitated glance.

'What is it with you two?' Jasmine asked in frustration. 'You're acting unusually weird all of a sudden.'

'Darling—' her mother used the soothing tone she saved for emergencies '—of course we're not acting weird! We're both looking forward to seeing you happily married to Mr...I mean Connor, aren't we, Elias?'

Her father grunted and picked up the sermon notes he'd

been revising before his wife and daughter had interrupted him.

'I'll be in the breakfast room,' he said and closed the door behind him.

Jasmine looked at her mother.

'Mum?'

Frances Byrne gathered up the patchwork quilt she was making for the parish fair.

'Don't worry about your father,' she said, folding the quilt haphazardly. 'He's nervous about the synod, that's all.'

Jasmine sighed. 'I understand, Mum, I really do.'

'No, you don't,' her mother said, clutching her needlework to her chest like a shield. 'That's the whole trouble; you don't understand.'

Her mother left the room and Jasmine was left staring at the space she'd just vacated, her mind swirling with a kaleidoscope of doubt and fear.

Connor called on her the Monday before the wedding. She'd not long come home from the clinic after a particularly trying day when one of her 'hopefuls' had slipped through the hoop and gone back on the streets for 'a fix'.

She was in no mood to discuss weddings, parties or anything.

'What do you want?' she sniped as she thrust her key in the lock.

He followed her into the flat, deftly catching her bag as she flung it to one side carelessly.

'Hard day at the office?' he commented, hanging her bag over the back of the nearest chair.

She shot him a fiery look, frightened that if she relinquished her anger she'd howl like a baby instead. Ever since that strange exchange with her parents she'd felt on edge, as if she were on the cusp of some new change in her life, a change that would be both permanent and painful.

'Why are you here?'

'I've missed you.'

She gritted her teeth. 'I wish you wouldn't make fun of me all the time.'

'I'm not. I'm telling you the truth. I really missed you today.'

'You saw me three days ago.'

'I like seeing you every day.'

'Why?' She glared at him. 'So you can inspect the goods daily to make sure you aren't being short-changed?'

His dark eyes flashed a gentle but firm warning.

'Are you premenstrual?'

'*What?*' she gasped.

'Are you—'

'I heard you the first time!' She stomped to the other side of the tiny lounge and, crossing her arms over her chest, faced him. 'Why is it that women's anger is nearly always relegated as hormonal? Why can't women be allowed to be angry without a biological reason?'

'What are you angry about?'

'Everything.' She let out her breath in a rush.

'That's pretty broad.' He perched on the edge of her old sofa. 'Want to narrow it down a bit?'

She was close to tears and hated him for it. She turned her back and addressed the dismal brown curtains with the silver fish holes in them.

'One of my clients went back on the streets last night,' she said, her voice sounding hollow and defeated. 'No one can find him.'

'Then how do you know he's back on the streets?'

She turned to look at him. 'We have it on reasonably good authority he bought some drugs at about midnight. No one has seen him since.'

'Has someone checked where he lives?'

'He doesn't really live anywhere.' She sighed heavily. 'Occasionally he stays overnight at one of the homeless hostels, but...'

'It's hard to believe that in this western civilisation of ours, people still choose to live on the streets,' he commented.

'It's not a choice!' She rounded on him hotly. 'Oscar's family kicked him out when he was barely fourteen! His step-father abused him repeatedly and his mother is an alcoholic. He'd been on the streets for three years before we came across him and began counselling him, to help him kick his heroin habit.'

'With any success?'

She sighed again. 'He'd agreed to go on a methadone pro-gramme but he's got a lot of anger stored up and whenever things get him down he has a relapse.'

'You really care about these people, don't you?' His ques-tion brought her head back up.

She met his eyes across the room and was surprised to find warmth in their depths.

'Yes, I do care.'

'So you work with them for next to nothing to do your bit to change the world?'

She hunted his face for signs of criticism but his expression remained largely impassive.

'I don't need a lot of money,' she answered.

'What about clothes?' His eyes ran over her worn jeans and faded pink T-shirt.

'I'm not a fashion follower.'

'Don't you ever wish you had what your sisters have?'

She found his question unsettling.

'My sisters finished their education. I didn't. Employment for me has been difficult.'

'Why didn't you finish your education?'

'Why all these questions?' she fired at him. 'You read the story in the press of how I nearly ruined Roy Holden's teach-ing career. You don't need to hear it all again from me.'

'On the contrary, I'd very much like to hear it from you.'

She was angrier than she'd ever been at being so cornered.

'It's an old story.' She gave him a blistering look. 'A

young, impressionable sixteen-year-old student spends too much time with one of her teachers. We were caught in what the witness claimed to be ''a compromising situation''. He was transferred to another school, his career prospects in shreds.'

'And you?'

She lowered her eyes. 'I left school the same day. I couldn't bear the furtive looks and whispered comments, so I quit.'

'Why are you still punishing yourself after all this time?'

Her eyes flew to his once more. 'I'm not punishing myself.'

'You were a child,' he said. 'You shouldn't have been cast as the wrongdoer if it was Roy Holden.'

'Roy Holden wasn't any such thing!' Her protestation was vehement. 'He did nothing wrong, nothing.'

Connor looked at her intently for a long moment.

'So you took the rap?'

She looked away. 'It was my fault.'

'Teenage girls are notorious for harmless flirting. It's natural.'

'I didn't flirt with him,' she said. 'I…I liked listening to him. He was knowledgeable and made the books we read come to life. I'd never had a teacher like him before. From the first moment he looked at me, I felt as if a part of me had come alive, and…' She suddenly realised how much she'd given away and clamped her mouth shut.

What was it about Connor Harrowsmith that made her speak so unguardedly?

'What was your parents' reaction when your relationship with Holden became public?' he asked after a stretching silence.

'They were devastated.' She sat down on the chair opposite. 'Especially my mother. She had a migraine for three days. My father simply brushed up on all his moralising lectures on why good Christian girls shouldn't give in to the temptation of fleshly desires and delivered them at every available opportunity.'

'But you hadn't, had you?' His dark eyes never left hers for an instant. 'Given in to fleshly desires,' he clarified when she remained silent.

She felt two flags of colour on her cheeks.

'Certainly not with Roy Holden,' she said. 'But after all the drama, as an act of rebellion, I had a one night stand with the captain of the football team.'

'And?'

She gave him a rueful look. 'It was dreadful.'

He smiled in empathy. 'My first time was a shocker too.'

She felt a smile tug at her mouth and quickly suppressed it. 'What did Mrs Holden say in the television interview?' she asked.

'Just that she supported her husband in his claim of innocence of any impropriety.'

''Did she say anything about me?'

'Not really.'

'Nothing at all?'

'Nothing too damning, if that's what's worrying you, but I think our marriage will definitely put out the remaining embers of gossip.'

Jasmine gnawed at her bottom lip. 'It was all so long ago. Eight years, in fact. I can't understand why anyone would be in the least bit interested after all this time.'

'Your father's a bishop,' he pointed out. 'Anything any member of his family does or has done is fuel for gossip. If he were a milkman no one would be interested.'

'I guess you're right.'

'Come on.' He got to his feet. 'Let's find somewhere to have a quick meal and then we can take a drive around the haunts you think your young absconder might be frequenting.'

Jasmine picked up her bag from where he'd placed it earlier and followed him to the door, all the time her feelings for him undergoing a rapid turnaround. Apart from her colleague, Todd, at the clinic she didn't know of a single man who'd willingly take out a weeknight of his time to trawl the down-trodden end of town to look for a person he didn't even know.

It made her see him in a totally different light.

It made her hatred retreat to a place where she could no longer access it.

It made her afraid.

After trawling the streets for an hour or so they stopped to share a Chinese meal in a small café in Chinatown. Jasmine picked at her food, her eyes avoiding Connor's across the small table.

'Are you nervous about Friday?' he asked after a few minutes of silence between them.

'Why should I be nervous?' She lifted her gaze to his, her chin slightly raised. 'It's not as if it's a real marriage, it's merely a formality so we both get what we want. I want to get my parents off my back and you want to secure your late mother's trust fund.'

He watched her face for endless seconds.

'I have every intention for this to be a proper marriage, Jasmine, and you know it.'

'You can hardly force me.' Her chin went a little higher.

A small smile lifted one corner of his mouth.

'No, but I have some persuasive tricks in my repertoire that should have the desired effect.' He picked up his wine. 'They haven't let me down in the past.'

She could feel the heat rise in her cheeks as she imagined him in the arms of God knew how many women, all of them gasping for the release only he could provide with his masterful mouth and intensely male body.

She covered her discomfiture with sarcasm.

'I suppose you're leaving a veritable legion of disappointed women behind you now that you're so intent on removing yourself from bachelordom?'

'Not as many as you probably think.' He smiled. 'But enough to make you jealous.'

'I'm not jealous!' Her insistence was perhaps a little too emphatic and she could tell from the glint in his eye he'd noted it.

'Of course you're not.' He leant back in his chair and surveyed her flushed features in a leisurely manner. 'You'd have to care about me to be jealous, wouldn't you?'

Without answering, she poked at a grain of rice with the end of her chopstick.

'How many lovers have you had?' he asked after a little pause.

She squashed the grain of rice before lifting her eyes to his.

'Not as many as you probably think but enough to make you jealous,' she threw his own answer back at him.

His dark eyes twinkled with amusement as he twirled his wine glass in his hand.

'Nice come-back. I'm impressed.'

She toyed with her own glass, her fingers restless and fumbling.

'It wasn't a come-back, it's the truth. No man wants to hear the intimate details of his future wife's past sexual exploits.'

'I don't know.' He put his glass down and leaned his elbows on the table to look at her closely. 'I think I'd be very interested to hear who's been in your bed.'

Hot colour suffused her face and she turned away to disguise it. He had seen too much as it was, and it wouldn't do to be too transparent; her pride would never survive it.

The waiter came to clear their plates and she was saved from having to respond. They declined dessert and, after the bill came and was settled, Connor got to his feet and, taking her arm, tucked it through his.

'Come on, where shall we look for Oscar now?'

Jasmine walked with him back along the streets of Darlinghurst and King's Cross, occasionally stopping to talk to someone she knew, but all the time she was conscious of Connor's arm linked through hers.

No one seemed to know where Oscar was, or if they did

they weren't saying. They'd walked back and forth along the main thoroughfares and into some of the less frequented ones. Even Connor began to balk as someone looking a little the worse for wear leered at Jasmine, making an obscene comment about her availability and price.

He quickly ushered her back into the brighter lights of the main street and, standing under the nearest street-light, frowned down at her.

'I want you to promise me you won't ever come here again by yourself. Do you promise?'

She met his determined gaze, her expression undaunted.

'Don't be silly, that was only Reggie. He's totally harmless, and besides—' she gave him a reassuring half-smile '—that was just the sweet sherry talking.'

'Sherry or not,' he growled as he led her back to his car, 'this place isn't even safe for the police, let alone civilians.'

'Are you frightened?' She gave him a teasing glance.

He glowered down at her, but she could see behind the frowning expression the glint of amusement in his eyes.

'Of course I'm not frightened, but I don't like the thought of you out here wandering amongst goodness knows what desperadoes.'

'They're people like you and me, Connor,' she said, her tone now serious. 'They've just made a couple of bad choices here and there. Any one of us could end up the same, given similar circumstances.'

He looked at her speculatively for a long moment before sighing. 'You're right, of course.' He took her arm again and continued walking the two blocks back towards his car.

Somehow she sensed a certain quality in his statement, as if he himself had at some point been in difficult circumstances but had managed to right himself. She realised with a prickle of conscience that she still hadn't asked him anything about his family. Most of the conversations they'd had about family members had concentrated on hers.

'What was your mother's name?' she asked, when they were back in his car.

He shot her a quick glance before turning back to start the engine.

'Ellen.'

'Do you remember her?'

'A bit.' His voice was gruff.

'What sorts of things do you remember?'

His car lurched forward with a jerk as if he'd let the clutch out too early.

'What is this?' His look towards her was frowning. 'Why the sudden interest in my background?'

'I was just making conversation.' She folded her arms defensively. 'You ask me intimate questions all the time so I don't see why I shouldn't do the same to you.'

'My mother has been dead for nearly thirty years,' he said after a tight little silence. 'I don't see any point in bringing it all up now.'

'I'm sorry.'

'Look.' He turned the car into the kerb and once it was stationary faced her. 'The script of my family doesn't exactly read like the happy families on TV.'

Even in the subdued lighting within the car she could see the normally handsome lines of his face grow harsh in remembrance.

'For most of my childhood it was a fight for survival,' he said. 'I couldn't wait to get away.'

'What about Finn?' she asked. 'Weren't you two ever close?'

His eyes hardened. 'Finn's my stepbrother, the child of Julian and Harriet. No blood relationship to me and I don't think a day went past without one or both of my step-parents reminding me of it.'

'It must have been so lonely for you.'

'Probably no lonelier than for you,' he said, his tone softening as he turned the car back into the traffic once more.

'What do you mean?' She gave him a narrow-eyed glance.

'It can't have been easy for you, surrounded by sisters who couldn't do a thing wrong.'

'I wasn't bad all the time.'

'You didn't need to be,' he said. 'Just being different was bad enough.'

Jasmine felt a trickle of alarm slide down her spine.

'W…what do you mean by that?'

He flicked another quick glance, taking in the tight clench of her hands in her lap, the worried look in her blue eyes and the anxious set of her slim body, sitting upright in the seat.

'I mentioned to you before that you don't seem to really belong in your family. Does that worry you?'

'I'm not a believer,' she answered quickly, 'in a church family. That is about as isolating as you can get.'

'The black sheep, eh?'

'You'd better believe it.' She tried to make her tone light to cover her unease at his probing questions.

'Good for you,' he said, surprising her yet again. 'Good for you.'

Jasmine opened her mouth to say something in return but just then she noticed a familiar figure out of the corner of her eye.

'Stop the car!' she cried.

'What?' Connor braked and she lurched forward. 'Here?'

She already had the door open and was half out before the car had completely stopped.

He watched as she disappeared down a dark alley off the main drag of The Rocks. He quickly parked in a loading zone, hoping his car wouldn't be towed away for contravening the parking restrictions, even though it was getting on for one a.m. in the morning.

He found her at the end of the alley with her arms around a scraggy-looking youth who smelt as if he'd recently been sick.

'Should we get an ambulance?' he asked.

She shook her head. 'He's fine, just a bit of a hangover.'

He helped her get the youth on his feet, carefully sidestepping what appeared to be the recently evacuated contents of his stomach on the cobblestones.

'Where to now?' he asked, looking at Jasmine.

'We'll have to take him to the hostel.'

'In my car?' He winced at the thought of whatever else was left in the lad's stomach waiting to make an untimely appearance on the leather interior.

'Of course in your car.' She hitched the boy's floppy arm across her shoulder and then eyeballed Connor with an accusing eye. 'Unless you'd rather not?'

Somehow he sensed it was some sort of test.

'My car it is.' He took the boy's other arm and half carried, half dragged the lad to his less than three months old, showroom perfect Maserati.

The hostel was a short drive away and as they hauled the lad inside a large man of Maori extraction greeted Jasmine warmly.

'Hey, girl. So you found him, eh?'

Jasmine handed over her young charge, who was mumbling something unintelligible as he flopped on the nearest chair and dropped his head between his knees. She absently stroked his straggly hair as she spoke to the hostel supervisor.

'I don't think he's had a fix, just a little too much to drink. He'll probably sleep it off.'

'I'll get the Doc to give him the once over. Just in case.'

'Thanks, Rangi.' She smiled up at him and then, turning to Connor, introduced them.

'Rangi, this is Connor Harrowsmith.'

The men shook hands and exchanged one or two comments about the All Blacks rugby team, which made them both laugh.

Jasmine watched the little exchange with interest. She hated to admit it but Connor wasn't exactly as she'd assumed he'd be. There was no sign of snobbery about him and he seemed at ease talking with anyone, from members of the clergy like her father to street kids, and those who looked after them, like Rangi. Just when she thought she'd got him all figured out he'd say or do something that would totally surprise her.

'You two want a coffee or something?' Rangi asked, glancing between them.

'Not this time.' Connor spoke for both of them. 'Jasmine's had a long day and I've got an early flight in the morning. Thanks, anyway.'

'No problem.' Rangi held out his hand once more. 'Come back some time and I'll show you round the place.'

'I'd like that.' Connor smiled and reached for Jasmine's hand. 'Come on, honey, let's get you home.'

She waited until they were outside before she spoke.

'Where are you flying to in the morning?'

He drew her closer to his side as a wobbling couple came towards them, the young woman tottering on impossibly high heels as her inebriated partner sang at the top of his voice.

He waited until they were well past before answering.

'I'm flying to Perth for two days, then to Adelaide, but don't worry, I'll be back in time for the wedding.'

Her heart sank at the thought of facing the rest of the week without him to banter with; she'd become so used to it she almost craved it now.

'Is there anyone you'd like to invite to the ceremony?' he asked as they came to his car.

She shook her head.

'I told you before: no guests, no photographs.'

He frowned as he deactivated the central locking.

'But what about friends, or a favourite relative, perhaps?'

She looked away. 'My mother's an only child and my father hasn't spoken to his younger sister in decades.'

He quirked one brow. 'Some sort of family feud?'

She gave a little shrug.

'I don't know. Ever since I can remember the topic of Aunt

Vanessa has been out of bounds. Apparently she did the unforgivable and brought shame on the Byrne name.'

'Like you?' His eyes held hers for a moment.

She returned his look without blinking.

'Yes,' she said. 'Just like me.'

He opened the door for her and she slipped under his arm to take her seat, her awareness of him intensifying a hundredfold as his hand lifted a lock of her trailing hair out of the way of the door just before he closed it.

She was silent on the journey back to her flat, Connor driving the short distance without even glancing once in her direction. She wondered if he was thinking about their wedding ceremony in four days' time and whether he had even half the misgivings she currently harboured about the union, or if he was secretly congratulating himself on finally bringing about a solution to his deceased mother's estate. His future would now be secure with a token wife in tow, while he carried on with his life just as he had before. It wasn't as if it were a love match; he'd made no promises to her and nor did she expect him to. When it came down to it, she hardly knew him, she realised with a little jolt when she sneaked a covert glance his way. What was going on inside that handsome, dark-haired head? What was he seeing from behind those dark brown eyes?

Her eyes lowered to his hands where they were resting on the steering wheel and she gave a tiny shiver. What were those hands planning to do once they had placed a wedding ring on her finger?

CHAPTER FIVE

IT ONLY took Jasmine half a day to pack her things ready to move into Connor's house. She sat back on her heels and sighed as she surveyed her five cardboard cartons on the floor in front of her. Her few meagre belongings wouldn't be taking up too much space in his Woollahra mansion but she refused to be ashamed. It had been her choice to live simply and just because she was marrying into the Harrowsmith family didn't mean she was going to rush out and buy a whole lot of designer wear.

Connor had organised a key for her and arranged for a removal firm to pick up her things while he was in Perth. Jasmine had just as quickly cancelled the removal van and caught a cab instead.

When she arrived with her things in the cab, it was the first time she'd seen his house. She was glad he was interstate so she could look around at her leisure, hoping she would learn something about the enigmatic man she was marrying in less than four days.

It was a big house but not really pretentious in either size or décor. The cab driver carried her things to the foyer for her and once he'd gone she closed the door and looked around.

The long, wide hallway had various doors leading off it and a Persian runner lined the floor over highly polished floorboards. A grandfather clock was ticking rhythmically in the background and a wide staircase wound itself in a half turn to the floor above.

Jasmine went to the first door and looked in. It was a large sitting room, tastefully appointed, comfortable sofas and stylish lighting with beautiful formal cream curtains at the bay windows. Again the polished floorboards were occasionally interrupted with Persian rugs, which looked as if they were velvet.

She went to the next room where she found a long cedar dining table with seating for at least twenty, the beautifully carved chairs each in themselves like works of art. The colour of the dining room walls was a dark forest green and the curtains at the windows a rust-coloured fabric with a gold edging.

The kitchen wasn't large but it was decorated all in white, giving it the appearance of space, and the high-tech appliances added to the overall affect of functionality.

She wandered through each of the remaining downstairs rooms, noting the tastefully decorated bathrooms, and the utility room near the back door which led out to a neatly landscaped garden, resplendent in the golds and reds of autumn from the various European trees situated there.

She left the upper floor till last. The closer she got to the main bedroom the more uncomfortable she became. She knew Connor was out of town and not likely to find her in his room but even as she cautiously opened the door she felt his dark eyes following her every movement even though he was at least a couple of thousand kilometres away.

His room was dominated by a huge bed, the linen of a caramel tone with white edging. There was one large rug which almost covered the entire floor except for a border of about a foot all round where the floorboards shone through.

A door to the right led to an *en suite* bathroom and, tempted as she was to check if there were any wet towels on the floor, she somehow resisted the urge to peek. Another door led to a walk-in wardrobe and, this time giving in to the temptation, she went in and looked at his clothes hanging in neat rows.

It was like being in the room with him.

She could even detect his distinctive male smell, a combination of a particular brand of aftershave and his own masculine scent. Almost of its own volition her hand went out and touched one of his shirts, holding the sleeve against her face, breathing in the fragrance, imagining his arms coming around her and...

'Looking for somewhere to hang your things?' His deep voice sounded behind her.

Jasmine swung around so quickly the shirt she'd been holding came off its hanger and landed in a heap at her feet.

'I...I thought you weren't coming back until tomorrow?' She knew her face was aflame for the walk-in wardrobe suddenly felt over-hot, as if someone had turned on a heater to full power.

'The Adelaide meeting was cancelled at the last minute.' His eyes flicked to his shirt on the floor.

She bent to pick it up, her fingers fumbling over the task of replacing it on the hanger. She hung it back with the rest of his shirts before facing him.

'My... My things are downstairs,' she stammered. 'I...I wasn't sure where you wanted me to put them.'

His expression was so hard to read in the soft light of the wardrobe. She felt increasingly uncomfortable in the small space, and her breathing instantly became shallow and hurried.

'There's plenty of room in here.' He reached past her and pushed the left row of his suits out of the way. 'Put what you can here and I'll have my housekeeper clear some space in the drawers later.'

While he was rearranging his clothes, Jasmine took the opportunity to back out of the wardrobe.

He followed her out and looked down at her standing before him with her bottom lip caught between her small white teeth.

'Will you have a problem sharing my wardrobe?' he asked.

'No.' She let her lip go. 'I have a problem sharing your bed.'

'But that's what married couples do,' he pointed out with a mocking twist to his mouth.

'But our...' she hesitated over the word '...marriage isn't going to be like an ordinary marriage.'

'How so?'

'I don't want to complicate things by sleeping with you.'

'Listen, honey.' His tone was dry. 'It will complicate things a whole lot more if you don't.'

'It seems so...so cold-blooded. We're practically strangers and we don't have any feelings for each other.'

'I don't know about that,' he drawled. 'I certainly feel something for you.'

She gave him a frosty look.

'Now you're making fun of me again. You can't possibly feel anything for me other than lust and I despise you for it.'

'Is that so?' His dark eyes glittered.

'Yes.' Her mouth was tight. 'I despise you for taking advantage of my...my little mistake and allowing it to go this far. One word from you and the baying hounds of the press would've gone elsewhere looking for blood, but no, you let them run me to the ground.'

'Perhaps I should point out that I have absolutely no control over what the press says or does. I was hounded myself as soon as I touched down in Perth and it was a hundred times worse at Mascot when I landed an hour ago.'

'Why?'

'It seems the marriage of a notorious playboy to a bishop's daughter sells papers. Everyone wants an exclusive. You only have to look outside if you don't believe me.'

Jasmine frowned and, hesitating for half a minute, moved across to the windows and looked down.

'Oh, my God!' She swung back around to face him. 'There must be twenty journalists out there!'

'I know.' His expression was rueful. 'And I've just told each and every one of them to go to hell.'

She sat on his bed and twisted her hands together in agitation. 'What can we do?'

He shrugged off his suit jacket and reached back inside the wardrobe for a hanger.

'Nothing until Friday. Once the marriage is finalised I think we'll be left alone.'

His eyes met hers across the room. 'Trust me, Jasmine. Our marriage will solve this little problem once and for all.'

Jasmine wondered if that were strictly true. Sure, it might resolve the public's interest in them and leave them to get on with their lives, but their marriage was going to produce some problems of its own, the first one being the increasing ambiguity of her feelings for him.

How was she supposed to keep them hidden? How was she supposed to walk away when she ceased to be useful to him, as was surely to happen at some time in the not too distant future?

How would she survive it?

She stayed where she was, perched on the edge of his bed, and watched as he unpacked his case, her eyes drinking in the sight of the muscles of his back as he bent to pick up something off the floor.

He turned suddenly and caught the tail end of her look and a teasing smile lit his eyes.

'Do your parents know we're going to be living in sin till Friday?'

She gave him an icy look and crossed her legs to stop the flow of heat from her lower body.

'We're not exactly living in sin,' she pointed out with as much primness as she could.

'No, more like living in lust,' he said, grinning.

'Don't be so ridiculous!' She crossed her arms as well.

He closed his suitcase and shoved it into the corner of the wardrobe before closing the door and leaning back against it with his customary indolence.

'Why does the thought of physical intimacy threaten you so much?'

She forced herself to meet his gaze.

'I'm not threatened; I just prefer to feel something other than hatred for my sexual partners.'

'If you truly hated me, Jasmine, you would've insisted on your father marrying us and preaching a forty minute sermon on the Seven Deadly Sins while he was at it.'

She felt a reluctant smile tug at her mouth and hastily looked away.

'What are the Seven Deadly Sins, by the way?' he asked.

She began rattling them off without thinking. 'Pride, wrath, envy, gluttony, avarice and…' She stopped and chanced a look at him.

'And?' he prompted with a glint in his dark eyes.

She sprang off the bed and stalked over to the window to see if the press had moved on, her back stiffly turned against his teasing smile.

'I can't stay locked up in here for the rest of the week,' she bit out. 'I just can't.'

She felt him move across the room to stand at her shoulder, with barely the width of a hair separating them.

She held her breath as his hand reached out to separate the curtains so he could inspect the scene below. The curtain fell back into place and he turned, his hands coming to rest on her shoulders as he looked down at her.

'The press gang has just about gone,' he reassured her. 'If we give it another half an hour it will be dark and we can go and have a meal somewhere in peace.'

She felt herself drowning in the chocolate pools of his eyes, the warmth of his hands penetrating the fabric of her top until she was sure his fingers would be permanently imprinted on her flesh.

She could feel the strength of his long thighs so close to hers, not quite touching, but her lower body already felt as if he was probing her intimately. She could feel the tug of her inner muscles preparing…anticipating…aching…

The sound of the telephone from the side of the bed broke

the moment. Jasmine wasn't sure whether to be relieved or annoyed at the intrusion.

'It's for you.' He handed her the extension and she took it from him with an unsteady hand.

'Hello?'

'Jasmine, it's Todd. Your mother told me I'd find you on this number. We need you at the clinic. Annie, that girl you've been working with, the one with the little kid, has been asking to see you for the past hour. I can't get rid of her and the kid is howling like a banshee. Casey called in sick and Rangi's got his hands full with two attempted suicides down at the hospital. Can you come?'

Her eyes met Connor's and she felt an unexpected sensation of warmth when she saw him reach for his car keys.

'I'll be there as soon as I can,' she promised and hung up the phone.

Connor pulled up outside the clinic and strode around to open her door.

'What time do you think you'll be finished?' he asked as she stepped out.

'I'm not sure.'

'Call me and I'll pick you up.'

'It might be very late.' She addressed the bottom of his chin, not wanting him to see the gratefulness in her eyes.

He tipped up her face with the end of one long, very male, finger.

'Call me, Jasmine. Promise.'

She felt her breath hitch in her chest as she held his unwavering gaze.

'I promise.'

He bent his head and sealed her mouth with his in a brief, hard kiss. Then, without another word, he stepped back from her to swing away to get back into his car.

She stood on the pavement as he deftly re-entered the traffic, listening to the roar of his powerful car as he skirted it around an off-loading cab, watching until his bright red tail-lights gradually disappeared into the distance.

One of her fingers went to her mouth and tentatively traced where his lips had been.

She dropped her hand and sighed as she turned to enter the clinic, but even hours later, whenever she sent her tongue out to moisten her lips, she was sure she could still taste him.

Annie Tulloch was clutching her young toddler to her chest when Jasmine entered her small office space. It was clear that, although the infant was now asleep, he hadn't been for all that long, judging from the tracks of tears down his grubby little face. It was also evident from the harried look on the young mother's face that this was not going to be a simple social call.

'I'm not using anything if that's what you're thinking,' she said even before Jasmine had shut the door.

Jasmine drew her chair close and sat down, touching the young woman on her thin arm encouragingly.

'I didn't think that at all. I know how determined you are now for Jake's sake. You've done so well, I'm very proud of you.'

Tears glittered in the young woman's eyes as she bent her head to her son's ruffled dark curls.

'Wade's coming out of jail,' she gulped. 'I know he'll come for us, I just know it.'

Jasmine drew in a painful breath. Wade Evert's criminal record already contained three accounts of domestic assault; she had no doubt he would have no hesitation in adding a fourth.

'What about the women's refuge?' she asked. 'You'd be safe there for a few days until the authorities inform you of his movements.'

'I came here from there,' Annie said. 'They're totally full. There wasn't even sleeping room on the floor.'

Jasmine chewed the end of her nail as she considered the possibilities.

'What about another suburb?' She reached for the telephone. 'I'll do a quick ring around to find a place for you and Jake.'

Even as she dialled the numbers she knew it was hopeless. Refuge places were few and far between. With the government dollar being squeezed so tightly, people like Annie and little Jake stood very little chance of being placed on priority. Annie's drug use history worked against her as surely as her dark colouring. It made Jasmine's blood boil at the injustice of it all.

After eight calls she put the telephone down in disgust. She drummed her fingers on the desk in front of her for a moment or two before snatching up the receiver again and quickly stabbing at the numbers.

The telephone seemed to ring for ages before it was picked up.

'Father?'

'Oh, Jasmine.' Her father's tone sounded somewhat distracted. 'Can I call you back? We're just in the middle of a prayer meeting. We should be through in about half an hour or so.'

She gritted her teeth. 'No, don't bother. It was nothing.'

She put the phone down and looked at the exhausted young mother in front of her.

'Will you excuse me for a minute?' she asked, pushing out her chair to get up. 'I need to make a private call. I won't be long.'

Annie nodded as she cuddled into her sleeping son's form, each and every sharp angle of her body defeated with tiredness.

Jasmine used the staff room extension and dialled Connor's number.

He answered on the second ring. 'Finished already?'

She couldn't help thinking his voice sounded disgustingly cheery considering the late hour. But then, she reminded herself, he'd probably been relaxing with his feet up on the plush leather sofa with a drink in one hand while she'd been fighting her way through a bureaucratic nightmare.

'No, I think this is going to be an all nighter.'

'Can I do anything to help?' he asked.

'Not unless you can find a safe house for a young mum and her toddler for a few days,' she said with a sigh.

'No room at the inn?' he quipped.

She was glad he couldn't see the way the corners of her mouth lifted in a reluctant smile.

'No room anywhere, I'm afraid.'

'What about a hotel?'

'My client hardly has enough money to feed her little boy let alone pay for a hotel.'

'What about a women's refuge centre?' he offered.

'I've rung all the ones in our area and they're all full.'

There was a small silence.

Jasmine suddenly felt embarrassed about calling him. She didn't really understand why she had, except somehow she'd felt as if she'd needed to hear the sound of his voice.

'Leave it with me.' His deep voice broke across her thoughts. 'I'll get back to you in half an hour or so, OK?'

'You don't have to get involved,' she said. 'This is my problem, not yours.'

'Then why did you ring me?'

'I...'

Her hesitation gave him all the answer he needed.

'Come on, admit it, Jasmine, you rang me because you need me.'

He was closer to the truth than he probably realised, she thought, even as she vehemently denied it.

'I don't need you. I can handle this on my own. I only rang to let you know I won't be home so you wouldn't wait up.'

She heard his soft chuckle of amusement and ground her teeth.

'I mean it, Connor.'

'Sure you do.'

'I'm hanging up.'

'Go right ahead.'

'And don't ring me back, I'm busy.'

'I won't.'

Her finger hesitated over the cut-off button. 'And I won't be back tonight.'

'That's fine.'

'You…you don't mind?' Uncertainty crept into her voice.

'Why should I mind?'

'But…but I thought you…'

'Listen, baby.' His sexy tone sent a shiver up her spine. 'In less than three days you'll be spending every night in my bed. I know it's hard, but if I can wait so can you.'

'I didn't mean that!'

He gave another deep laugh. 'Sure you didn't.'

'Go to hell!'

'I'm well on my way, or so your father told me not so long ago.'

'I don't think even hell is going to be hot enough for you,' she spat back.

'It certainly won't be if you're not there with me,' he teased.

She opened her mouth to throw back a stinging retort but he'd already hung up.

She glared at the telephone for half a minute, fighting the temptation to call him back just so she could have the last word, but a sound from the next room reminded her of her responsibilities to her client.

Annie turned in her chair when Jasmine came back in.

'Have you found somewhere for us to go?'

'Not as yet.' She held out her arms for the little boy who'd just woken. 'But I'm still working on it.'

The toddler stopped snivelling as soon as Jasmine cuddled him close to her chest. She stroked his little back as she sat on the edge of her desk, breathing in the soft baby smell of him as his tiny fingers curled around a strand of her hair.

'Annie, have you considered contacting your mother?'

Annie's expression closed over.

'Why should I? She gave me away when I was four years old. What sort of mother is that?'

'I understand how you feel, especially since you're now a mother yourself, but a few years ago things weren't all that easy for a single mother.'

'They're not easy now,' Annie put in dejectedly.

'I know, but your mother did what she thought was best at the time. You can't blame her for trying to give you the best chance.'

'I can manage on my own.' Annie's face was determined. 'I've had to ever since I was fourteen.'

Jasmine sighed. Annie was one of the saddest cases she'd ever had to deal with. Every time she took a couple of steps forward something would come along and send her three steps backwards.

Todd had warned her not to get so involved. Professional distance, he called it, but there was something about Annie Tulloch that had touched Jasmine from their first meeting. She wasn't exactly sure what it was about the fragile young woman that stirred her so much. Most of the street kids she worked with had similar tragic backgrounds and yet Annie had slipped under her professional guard right from the start.

Little Jake gave Jasmine's hair another tug and gurgled up at her.

'Hey, little guy,' she said, tickling him under the chin. 'Don't you know that's no way to treat a lady?'

'It certainly isn't,' said a very familiar male voice from the door.

Jasmine swung around to see Connor standing there with a take-away food bag in one hand and a hot drinks tray balanced in the other.

'Anyone for coffee?' he asked, stepping into the room.

It was clear from the look on Annie's face as she eyed the

paper bag he set before her that it had been quite some time since she'd eaten.

'I got chicken nuggets for the little one.' He took out the small container and handed it to Jasmine before turning back to Annie. 'I'm Connor, by the way. Jasmine's fiancé.'

Annie's eyes widened before turning to Jasmine.

'You're getting married?'

Jasmine gave a chicken nugget to Jake before answering.

'Yes…on Friday.'

'I thought you didn't believe in marriage?' Annie said, popping a French fry into her mouth.

'She's a very recent convert, aren't you, darling?' Connor smiled.

Jasmine sent him a quelling look before handing Jake another nugget.

'I've found accommodation for you, by the way,' Connor announced.

'You have?' Jasmine and Annie spoke in unison.

'As safe houses go this has got to be one of the safest. Beryl Hopper has spent the last twenty odd years looking after folk who need a break to get back on their feet. And don't be fooled by the blue rinse hair and the grandmotherly figure; she's got a black belt in just about every version of martial arts. No one but no one will get past her unless she says so.'

'I don't know what to say.' Annie smiled up at him shyly.

'Where does this Beryl woman live?' Jasmine asked.

'In the Blue Mountains.' He checked his wristwatch. 'She should be here shortly. She was visiting a friend in town but I managed to track her down before she left.'

'There are formalities to see to,' Jasmine said. 'I have to get police clearance and so on.'

Connor reached for the toddler who had held up his arms towards him.

'You do what you need to do while this little chap and I finish off these fries.'

Jasmine reached for the phone, trying not to notice how at ease he seemed to be with the little child.

A short while later Todd came to her office to announce the arrival of Beryl Hopper who within minutes had ushered Annie and Jake out to her car with the bustling efficiency of a mother hen.

Jasmine stood by Connor's side on the pavement and watched as the older woman's car drove off with an ignominious hiccough or two before merging into the late night traffic.

She felt his glance on her and faced him, meeting his eyes in the shadow cast by the streetlight.

'Thank you for what you did tonight.'

'It was nothing.'

She gave him a long, studied look.

'How did you meet Beryl Hopper?'

'She was a friend of my mother's,' he said with a fond smile. 'She's been there like a bull terrier in the backyard of my life making sure I don't go too far off the rails.'

'She's certainly had her work cut out for her then,' she said with an attempt at wry humour.

He looked down at her for a long moment without speaking, his dark gaze holding hers.

'You look exhausted.'

She gave a weary sigh as she lowered her eyes. 'I am.'

'Come on.' He put his arm around her shoulders and reached for his keys. 'Let's get you to bed where you belong.'

Jasmine didn't have the strength to argue with him about which bed she preferred to occupy.

Once in the car she closed her eyes and laid her head back against the soft leather upholstery, trying not to think about his hard-muscled thighs so close to hers, or about his strong, capable, long-fingered hands on the steering wheel.

Within a few minutes he pulled into his driveway and walked with her to the house, his arm still casually slung around her shoulders. She didn't move out of his hold, even though a part of her insisted she should.

He opened the door and let his arm drop as he tossed his keys on to the hall table.

'Do you want a drink or something?' he asked, shrugging his jacket off.

She hovered uncertainly, not sure what he was expecting of her.

'Hey.' He touched her cheek with one finger in a fleeting caress. 'Go to bed, sleepy eyes.'

'But—'

He pressed his finger to her lips. 'Goodnight, Jasmine.'

She turned and began treading the stairs, each and every step she took feeling like a marathon.

'I'll be in the spare room if you need me,' he said as she reached the upper landing.

She turned to look back down at him. She so wanted to say she didn't need him but it seemed like tempting fate to voice the very words that could in the end prove to be her downfall.

'Goodnight,' she said instead and took another step.

'Jasmine...'

Her hand stalled on the hand rail, her heart tripping over itself in her chest at the seductive sound of his voice.

'Yes?'

He seemed about to say something but then changed his mind.

'Nothing. It can wait. I'll see you in the morning.'

He turned and the study door closed behind him, the hall suddenly seeming empty without him.

Jasmine continued up the stairs and closed the bedroom door softly behind her, but even when she was curled up in the big bed a few minutes later she wondered what it would be like to sleep with his warm arms around her, their legs entwined, and his firm mouth on hers.

She pummelled the pillow and clamped her eyes shut but it was hours before she could relax enough to sleep.

When she woke the next morning there was a short note from Connor stating his absence due to a problem with one of his outlets in Brisbane. His hastily scrawled message informed her he would be back in time for the wedding.

She screwed up the note and threw it at the nearest wall. How like him to desert her just when she'd decided she needed him around!

Damn him!

CHAPTER SIX

IT SEEMED strange to Jasmine to be at a wedding where her father, in his whiter than white cassock, wasn't presiding over the proceedings, his booming voice echoing throughout the cathedral.

For one thing, the registry office wasn't big enough for a Bishop let alone an echo, and as she had insisted on no guests the ceremony was brief and impersonal.

She told herself she didn't mind. She wasn't the type to stand up in front of distant relatives, dressed like a meringue and feeling like every type of fraud for wearing a veil.

She was glad she'd worn a short bright red dress—very glad. She was the family tart, after all, so it seemed rather fitting.

However, when she first arrived, she caught Connor's eye and she felt a momentary flutter of unease at the glitter of anger in his eyes. She knew he was annoyed and his fury at her would be intensified by the fact that he couldn't speak to her about it until they were finally alone.

She hadn't been at his house the night before when he had returned from interstate. She'd left her own terse note informing him of her plans to spend the night with friends. She hadn't spent the night with anyone. She'd booked herself into a cheap hotel and spent the night eating her way through the mini bar chocolate supply, trying to convince herself she still had time to call it all off.

But she hadn't called it off.

She still wasn't sure why.

She wanted to put it down to her rebellious streak that insisted she do the exact opposite of what was expected of her, but deep down she knew it wasn't that at all.

When the celebrant gave permission to kiss the bride Jasmine was unprepared for the heat and fire of Connor's mouth on hers. It wasn't a kiss to seal a contract; it was a kiss to remind her she'd just tied herself to a man she barely knew, a man who held all the cards.

As soon as they left the registry office a huddle of photographers crowded around as they tried to get back to his car. Jasmine put her head down as he tugged her behind him, almost tripping over her own feet as she tried to negotiate the pavement in her high heels.

At last they were in the car, several camera lenses pressed right up against the windows even as Connor began to drive away.

There was a stiff silence until they'd made their way out of the main flow of traffic.

'I hope you've got a very good explanation,' he ground out as he deftly skirted around a driver trying to reverse park.

'I don't have to explain myself to you,' she bit back.

'Perhaps not, but have you thought of how your parents are going to feel when they see tomorrow's paper with you splashed all over the front of it dressed like a streetwalker?'

She hadn't given her family a thought and it made her resent him for pointing it out.

'I don't have an extensive wardrobe,' she said. 'I'll have you know this is my best dress.'

He gave her a look of frustration before turning back to the traffic slowing up ahead.

'Then why the hell didn't you tell me? I could've arranged for you to get some clothes. It's not as if I can't afford to dress you.'

'I thought your main intention was to get me out of my clothes.' She gave him a caustic glance.

'You know something?' He turned her way as the traffic came to a stop. 'You're one hell of a complicated young woman, do you know that?'

She folded her arms across her chest in a defensive pose.

'You surely didn't have to go to the length of marrying me to come to that conclusion, did you?'

His wry laugh broke the tension.

'No. I guess you're right; I didn't.'

'Then why did you?' She swivelled to look at him.

He gave her one of his long, studied looks before answering.

'It seemed like a good idea at the time.'

'And now?' She held his gaze without blinking.

'And now.' He put his foot back down on the accelerator as the traffic ahead began to move forwards. 'Now we've made our bed, so to speak, we're going home to lie on it.'

The car shot forward and she clutched at the armrest to steady herself. There was a promise in those dark eyes of his, and while she still didn't know him well, she did know that was one promise he was going to keep.

But he didn't take the turn-off to the eastern suburbs. Jasmine shot him a questioning glance as he headed for the freeway south.

'Where are we going?'

'I've got something to show you,' he answered. 'I got my housekeeper to pack a weekend bag for you.'

She wasn't sure what made her angrier—the fact that he'd instructed a housekeeper she'd somehow never met to go through her things or that he hadn't informed her of his plans for the weekend.

'Maria comes in a couple of times a week,' he said before she could fire up her stinging tirade. 'She doesn't speak much English but enough to tell me off for leaving my towels on the floor all the time.' He gave her a quick grin but she scowled back at him.

'I could've packed my own bag. I don't like other people going through my things.'

'You don't have all that much to go through,' he said dryly. 'But once we get back to town I'll make sure that's rectified.'

'If you think buying me a whole new wardrobe of clothes

is going to change anything, think again. If and when I want new clothes I'll get them myself.'

'With what?' He shot her a flinty glance.

She turned away from his probing eyes.

'I have some money, not the disgusting amount someone like you earns, but I manage.'

'You live like a bloody pauper!' he said. 'Why is that? Just so you can make the differences between you and your family even more marked?'

Jasmine tensed.

'I don't do anything of the sort. I just don't see the need for expensive clothes when there are kids on the streets without food and shelter.'

'Well, if those kids on the streets spent a little less on drugs and drink perhaps they would have somewhere to live and something to eat.'

She gave him a gelid glare.

'How typically middle class! You with your silver spoon still sticking out of the corner of your goddamned mouth!'

'Watch it,' he warned.

'You know people like you really make me sick,' she continued recklessly. 'You've never had to worry about where the next meal was coming from and yet you dare to criticise those who have nothing, not even a parent who loves them...' She stopped as she realised what she'd said. He'd grown up from the age of four without either of his parents and while he may never have had to worry about hunger she suspected love was something that had been in short supply.

'I'm sorry,' she mumbled. 'I shouldn't have said that. I wasn't thinking.'

'Forget it,' he said without glancing her way. 'I already have.'

He put his foot down and overtook four cars in one stretch. Jasmine stole a covert glance at him. His expression was inscrutable. However, she noticed his hands on the steering wheel were tense.

She felt terrible.

She sat in a miserable silence and wondered how she could apologise any further. She was used to his teasing, not his temper, and it made her realise how little she knew of him. She wished Sam had been back from her honeymoon so she could have asked her to fill her in. Surely being married to his stepbrother, Finn, would have given her some insight into his character?

After another silent half-an-hour Jasmine began to suspect where he was taking her—Pelican Head. He drove past her mother's friend's turnoff until he came to the end of the road to a large Victorian house. Jasmine had explored the grounds in the past, imagining it was haunted, with the shadowed windows of the old house looking like ghostly eyes as they surveyed whoever was game enough to trespass. Never in her wildest dreams had she ever expected to be driving up the pot-holed driveway with a new husband, bags packed to stay the weekend.

'I'll take our things inside,' Connor said. 'You want to have a look around by yourself for a while?'

How had he known she wanted to be alone just now?

'All right.' She avoided his eyes as she slipped off her high heels and pushed her feet into a pair of flat casuals.

He took their bags from the boot and made his way to the old house while she stood and breathed in the cooling evening air. The sun was sinking behind the screen of tall gum trees behind the house, casting rays of golden light across the iron-laced veranda.

She turned away from the house and walked towards the creek, where the soft sway of the she-oaks in the light breeze and the trickle of water over the river stones gradually began to calm her overstretched nerves.

She bent down to trail her fingers through the velvet softness of the maidenhair fern that was bowing towards the water and she breathed in the earthiness of moss and damp, a heady mix after the fumes of the bustling city.

So this was the first day of her married life.

She straightened and absently twirled the band on her finger, wondering if it would be there long enough to leave a mark.

It was certainly an unusual way to start a marriage. A rushed ceremony to satisfy her parents' need for propriety as well as to secure Connor's mother's estate, not to mention keeping the gossip-mongers at bay. It seemed a strange set of reasons for marriage, but then what else in her life wasn't strange? She was like a stranger in her own family. She looked different. She even felt different. All her life she'd felt as if some part of her was missing and, just like a small piece of a jigsaw, the picture wasn't complete.

It was nearly dark when she wound her way back through the bush to the old house.

Connor had turned on some lights, which took away from the haunted look she had been so used to seeing. In fact, the old house almost looked alive, as if it had been waiting all those years for someone to come along and switch on its lights so it could see through its dark windows again. Ever since she'd first skirted past the place on one of her walks she'd felt as if someone inside the house was watching her, but now it looked just as it was—a very old and rundown house in the middle of nowhere.

She shook her head at her musings and walked up the steps to the front door. When it opened in front of her she started and almost stumbled back down the steps.

'You look like you've just seen a ghost,' Connor said.

She covered her embarrassment with cynicism. 'I don't believe in the afterlife.' She made to brush past him but his arm came out to block her entry.

'Aren't I supposed to carry you over the threshold or something?' he said with a teasing light in his eyes.

She met his look with a hard light in her own.

'And aren't you supposed to love and cherish me till death us do part?'

His expression became unreadable as he dropped his arm.

'What I feel about you is irrelevant,' he said. 'What's more important is what you feel about yourself.'

She stared at him for a moment without speaking. Then, retreating into the protection of her usual sarcastic armour, she spat back at him, 'As much as we are both likely to regret it, you are my husband, not my psychoanalyst.'

'In that case I'd better carry you over the threshold.' Without any other warning, he scooped her up in his arms and carried her into the house.

'Put me down!' she shrieked, straining against him.

'When I'm ready.' He tightened his hold. 'Now stop struggling or I'll drop you.'

'I don't want you to—' Her words were suddenly cut off by his mouth coming over hers, stopping all sound.

She stopped fighting him and began fighting with herself— fighting to keep control of the yearning his kiss had ignited like a lighted taper to dry kindling. She was erupting into leaping flames of need; there wasn't a part of her untouched by the pressure of his mouth on hers. Her skin tingled all over, her heart leaping erratically when he deepened the kiss with a moist slide of his tongue through her parted lips.

The flames of need were now an inferno. She was aching for him inside and out, her arms tight about his neck, holding on as if he were the lifeline she needed to stay afloat in the sea of passion that was threatening to consume them both.

She felt him lower her feet to the floor, her body sliding down his erotically, snagging on the thrust of his aroused body, leaving her in no doubt of what he craved.

But then he lifted his mouth off hers and she opened her passion-glazed eyes to find him looking at her intently, a question lurking in the depths of his chocolate gaze.

She couldn't hold his gaze.

She pushed herself out of his hold, putting some much

needed distance between them. She couldn't think straight when his hands were on her, her thoughts becoming as jumbled and erratic as her pulse. She had no idea how she was going to get through the weekend without betraying herself; her physical desire for him was already spiralling out of her control just from one kiss!

She turned around and looked at the interior of the house rather than face his sardonic half-smile.

'What plans do you have for this place?' she asked casually as she picked at a flake of cracked paint on the nearest wall.

'I was hoping you'd help me with that.'

She glanced over her shoulder at him.

'I don't know anything about interior decorating.'

'But you're familiar with the house.'

She turned to face him.

'Before today I've never even stepped inside the place.'

He raised one brow. 'Not very neighbourly of you.'

'Look, I came to the shack down the road to escape, not to socialise with whoever may have been living here. Anyway, word has it the person who was last here was a recluse.'

'Weren't you even a little bit tempted to come over and look around?'

'No, why should I?' She gave him a reproachful glare. 'Unlike some, I do actually respect people's need for space.'

'But surely you must have wondered who was living here? I thought all women were by nature curious.'

Jasmine found his question slightly disturbing. The truth was she had been intensely curious about the occupant of the old house but her own need for peace had prevented her from investigating any further. She'd wandered through the grounds once or twice, watching for any signs of movement behind the half-drawn blinds before turning for the creek path that ran through the property.

'All I know is whoever lived here wasn't keen on home

maintenance,' she said with a wry glance towards the peeling paint.

'Yes, it does look a little neglected but I like a challenge.'

He wandered over to the bookshelves where books were lying haphazardly amongst decades of dust. He picked up a copy of Thomas Hardy's *Tess of the D'Urbervilles* and blew off a cloud of dust. 'I thought the place needed some attention and, like you, I was drawn to the solitude.'

Her eyes connected with his across the room but she felt as if something more than the meeting of gazes had passed between them.

She realised then that she knew virtually nothing about his work, what sort of stresses he had to contend with. In fact, apart from what she'd occasionally read in the press and what she'd heard from Finn and Sam he was an unknown quantity. The fact that she was now married to him made her ignorance all the more intimidating.

'Do you enjoy your work?' She was pleased with her question; it demonstrated an interest without revealing her need to pry.

He put the old book down and dusted off his hands.

'It pays the bills and creates a few more,' he answered. 'Like most jobs.'

'Business is like that,' she said in response.

'What about you?' he asked. 'Do you have plans to move on from the clinic to a job with more sociable hours?'

'No.' Her reply was short and sharp.

He gave her a studied look.

'You have an insatiable desire to be needed, don't you?' he observed. 'That's why you work yourself into the ground on a wage that wouldn't feed a sparrow.'

'I don't see how it's any business of yours what I do or how much I earn doing it.'

She turned away from his penetrating look and inspected the bookshelves nearest her. She picked up a copy of Milton's poems and flicked idly through the yellowed pages.

'What made you buy this house?' she asked.

She sensed his casual shrug but didn't look up at him as she put the book carefully back amongst the others.

'I liked the mystery of the place,' he answered. 'Mystery intrigues me.'

Just then the lights flickered momentarily, went out completely, and then came back on all within the space of a few seconds.

Jasmine felt a tiny shiver run through her as she turned to look at him.

'Are you frightened?' he asked, a half-smile lurking at the corner of his mouth.

'Of course not!' She gave her head a toss.

A distant roll of thunder sounded and she visibly flinched. His smile widened.

'Sounds like we're in for a storm.' He watched the interplay of emotions on her expressive face. 'Don't worry, I'll protect you.'

She didn't need to tell him her biggest fear was him, not the approaching storm; she was sure he must see it for himself in the widening of her eyes as he stepped towards her.

She held her breath as he touched her gently on the cheek with the back of his hand.

'Don't be frightened, Jasmine.' His voice was like velvet running over her skin.

'I...I'm not frightened.' Her voice caught in her throat. 'I just don't like storms.'

'What is it you don't like, the thunder or the lightning?'

'I don't like the unpredictability of it.' She swallowed. 'You never know when the next strike is going to come; they seem to come from a long way off and then the next moment it's right on top of you, catching you off guard.'

'Like falling in love?' His eyes held hers for a moment.

'I'm not sure. Anyway, what would you know of love? I thought a playboy's credo was to keep things strictly on a physical plane?' She knew disapproval coloured her tone but couldn't check it in time.

His mouth lifted in one of his characteristic half-smiles.

'Even playboys can fall in love,' he answered smoothly. 'And just like thunder and lightning it can take them completely by surprise.'

She felt increasingly uncomfortable under his watchful gaze and lowered her own to inspect the floorboards at her feet.

'How often have you fallen in love?' She hoped her tone suggested indifference.

'Not often enough to be any expert on the subject,' he said.

She didn't understand why his answer had disappointed her.

'What about you?' he asked into the stretching silence.

She would have answered him with some carefully framed, suitably evasive reply but just then a bolt of savage lightning split the sky, turning the room a sickly shade of electric-green. She flinched as if someone had struck her from behind and flung herself forward into his arms. He held her against him as the thunder boomed like a cannon over their heads, his hard body like a fortress against the enemy at the gates. She heard a crackle and the light flickered and then finally snuffed out like a candle in a sudden breeze.

She squeezed her eyes shut as another bolt of lightning rent the sky, closely followed by the roar of angry thunder.

'It's all right.' His hand stroked the back of her head. 'It'll pass in a few minutes.'

'It's getting so dark,' she said into his chest.

She felt rather than heard his rumble of amusement.

'It is, now that the power's off.'

'Do you have a torch?' Her tone was hopeful as she looked up at him.

His eyes were like fathomless pools as he held her gaze. She was suddenly conscious of the hard length of him against her, its presence between them a reminder of the intimacy of both their circumstances and relationship. They were totally alone, without the distraction of either people or power; alone in a big old house still trembling with a host of memories seeping through every wind-borne crack in the windows.

'I don't have a torch,' he said.

'A candle?' She peered up at him in the ever increasing darkness.

He shook his head.

'But I have laid a fire in the fireplace and I have some matches.'

She didn't see any point in disguising her relief.

'Thank God.' She gave a tiny shudder against him. 'For a moment I thought we were in big trouble.'

There was a strange little silence.

'We are in big trouble,' he said.

'What sort of trouble?' She looked up at him again.

'This sort of trouble,' he answered and bent his head to hers.

CHAPTER SEVEN

ANOTHER shaft of lightning filled the room momentarily with green-tinged light but once it flashed Jasmine didn't even spare a thought for the thunder. When Connor's mouth covered hers she was lost to the violence of the storm outside, her only thought on the storm of need he'd awakened inside her with the first dart of his tongue into her warm mouth.

She was carried along by the maelstrom of desire pulsing between them, a desire she didn't want to feel but couldn't stop herself from feeling. It was as if the force of nature had taken over her body, making her act in ways totally unfamiliar to her. Her hands were already threading their way through his dark hair, her soft whimpering cries filling the silence of the room as he left her mouth to blaze a trail of kisses down her neck. She was on a wanton path to destruction but she didn't care any more. She heard the rasp of the zip at the back of her dress and stepped out of its silken folds, glad of the cloak of darkness as she stood before him in her underwear.

She felt the scorch of his eyes even through the darkness.

'I'll light the fire,' he said in a whispering tone.

She wanted to tell him he'd already lit a fire; her body felt as if it were going to burst into leaping flames right then and there. But she said nothing as he searched along the top of the mantelpiece for the box of matches.

The strike of one against the side of the box seemed loud now that the storm outside had faded to a distant rumble. She watched as the tiny glow of the match cast his features into relief, giving him a rakish look. He bent to the laid fire and it erupted into a warm glow, giving her a timely reminder that he must have done this a hundred times with a hundred different women in a hundred different locations.

He reached for her but she'd anticipated the move and put the old sofa between them. The fire lighting him from behind made him appear larger and more threatening as he loomed over her, his eyes scorching her from head to toe.

'Cold feet, Jasmine?' he asked in his customary mocking tone.

She set her chin at a defiant angle.

'I'm not on the Pill.'

'I have a condom.'

'Only one?' Her look was cynical.

'I came prepared.' There was an intent light in his eyes that frightened her.

'I bet you did,' she sniped back at him as he made a move towards her. 'In an array of colours and textures, no doubt.'

'I always aim to please.'

She tore her eyes away from his and did another round of the sofa.

'Will you stop following me like some nasty predator?' she railed at him crossly as he closed the distance with another stride. She didn't trust herself not to throw herself back in his arms and so retreated behind a wall of cold anger to disguise her need. 'Leave me alone, Connor, or I'll scream.'

His eyebrow lifted in amusement.

'Who do you think is going to hear you? God?'

'Believe me—' she gave him a fulminating look '—when I scream the whole universe will hear it.'

'A screamer, eh?' His eyes danced as he looked her over once more.

She felt herself blush from head to foot at his double meaning. Well, that was one thing on which he could reassure himself; her responses were hardly going to wake the neighbours if her track record was anything to go by, she thought bitterly.

She crossed her arms over her chest, wishing she could reach her dress on the other side of the sofa.

As if reading her mind, Connor bent down and, picking it up, dangled it from his fingers.

'You want this?'

She tightened her mouth. 'I'm cold.'

'There's a roaring fire over here,' he said, pointing back over his shoulder.

She ignored his comment and commanded, 'Hand me my dress.'

'Come and get it.'

She met the challenge in his eyes and, taking a swift intake of breath, strode across and snatched it out of his hand. She turned her back to him and stepped back into it with as much grace as her fumbling fingers would allow. Once she was decently covered she faced him once more, the light of rebellion still firing in her eyes.

'If you thought you could haul me down here for a weekend of seduction think again. I won't be any man's plaything.'

'The thought never crossed my mind.'

She glared at his guileless expression.

'You're making fun of me again and I won't stand for it.'

He laughed softly as he turned back to stoke the fire behind him.

'Don't worry, Jasmine—' he addressed the settling flames '—I won't suddenly leap on you and take you without your consent. That's not my style.'

'No.' She tightened her hands into fists. 'Your style is more the sneak up and take them when they're off guard, isn't it?'

'So you do confess to being a little tempted?' He looked over his shoulder at her standing stiffly on the other side of the sofa. 'That is, when your guard is down?'

'No!' Her protestation was far too vehement, sounding more defensive than convincing. 'I'm not tempted at all, guard down or not.'

She could see he didn't believe her, his dark eyes communicating as surely as if he'd spoken the words out loud.

'I'm not interested in casual relationships,' she added when he didn't speak.

'Our relationship is hardly what I'd call casual,' he pointed out wryly. 'After all, we've already shared the same bed and are now officially married.'

'You're really enjoying this, aren't you?' she said. 'It really suits your perverse sense of humour to have me in this unspeakable situation, doesn't it?'

'I can't deny the element of comedy in the situation.'

'Comedy?' She almost shrieked the word. 'You think this funny, me being imprisoned with you in this haunted mausoleum all weekend?'

'I thought you didn't believe in the after-life?'

She gave a shiver as the old house creaked, as if in protest. 'I don't, but this place still gives me the creeps.'

'It's just an old unloved house, Jasmine. By the time we've finished, all the ghosts will be well on their way.'

She didn't care for the glint of mischief in his dark gaze and hastily turned her back to inspect the nearest object of furniture, to cover her unease. It was a small escritoire, beautifully crafted and in good condition considering the state of the house.

'It's a nice piece.' He spoke from behind her left shoulder. 'I bought it at an auction a few days ago.'

She admired his taste but didn't say so.

'I bought a few other things, which will be delivered on Tuesday.'

She turned to look at him at that.

'You're planning to stay until Tuesday?'

'As honeymoons go it's still rather short but I thought we needed more than two nights to get to know one another.'

'We'd need a century.' She brushed past him agitatedly to go and warm herself by the fire. 'That is if I felt so inclined to get to know you at all.'

'I think by the time we leave here you'll know me very well.'

She knew he was using the biblical meaning of the word by the element of lazy humour in his teasing tone.

'I don't want to know you. I don't even like you.'

'The reason you don't like anyone, including me, is because you don't even like yourself.'

She rolled her eyes at him.

'You can quit the Freud impersonation right now,' she said tightly. 'Analyse your own behaviour before you start on mine. You're the one who got us into this unholy mess in the first place.'

'You were the one in the wrong room,' he pointed out neatly.

She was infuriated by his satirical tone.

'I made a simple mistake! Am I supposed to pay for it for the rest of my life?'

He gave an indifferent shrug of one shoulder.

'That's entirely up to you.'

'What do you mean by that?' She stared at him suspiciously.

'I mean this "unholy mess" we're in, as you so indelicately described it, could turn out to be a whole lot of fun.'

'I'd rather die than have fun with you.'

He raised his eyebrows at her.

'Careful, such careless untruths could call that old storm right on back.'

'Don't be ridiculous.' Her tone was scathing.

There was a very definite grumble of thunder in the distance. Connor winked at her and she turned back to the fire, her face glowing more than the flames still leaping there.

'Would you like something to eat?' he asked.

'How can we cook without power?'

Just then the lights gave a tentative flicker or two before coming on completely.

Connor lifted his head towards the ceiling with a grin.

She didn't know what to say. She even wondered if he'd

engineered the whole black out thing to suit his plan for seduction.

He could see her scepticism and he smiled.

'Come on. Let's see what's in the kitchen to eat.'

She frowned as she followed him from the room at a safe distance. When she saw how well-stocked the old refrigerator was as well as the walk-in pantry she had to concede that he had certainly gone to a lot of trouble; at the very least, there was enough food to keep them going for a month.

'Would you like some wine?' He took a bottle out of the door of the refrigerator and held it up for her inspection.

She didn't normally drink much alcohol but decided that she would this time. She needed something other than him to stimulate her senses!

'All right,' she said.

She watched as he uncorked the wine, poured some into the two glasses he'd taken from a cupboard. She took the glass he held out to her and took a tentative sip.

He raised his own in a salute.

'To a happy union.'

She refused to join him in the toast.

He took a generous mouthful and she watched the movement of his neck as he swallowed. She dragged her eyes away and stared into the contents of her own glass for a long moment.

'You have to drink it, not wait for it to evaporate,' he said.

His mockery made her reckless. She gritted her teeth and, with the barest hesitation, lifted the glass to her lips and downed the contents in one hit. She put the glass down on the counter and met his taunting gaze.

'Another?' he asked.

'Why not?' she said, and pushed it towards him.

After topping up his own he refilled it for her, leant back against the counter top and surveyed her defiant pose.

'Doesn't do to drink on an empty stomach,' he cautioned.

'I can handle it.' She drained the glass with three mouthfuls.

He pursed his lips as he watched her.

'I can see what you're up to.' He twirled the glass in his hand. 'But you'll regret it in the morning.'

'So?' She tossed her head at him. 'If I fell for your seductive plans I'd regret it in the morning too. The way I see it, this is the lesser of two evils.'

'I have no plans for seduction. When we make love it will be because we both want it so badly there's no other choice.'

'There's always a choice.'

He quirked an eyebrow at her.

'That high moral ground is unfamiliar territory for you. I thought you enjoyed playing devil's advocate?'

'I'm having a night off.' She suppressed a hiccough and steadied herself against the counter as the alcohol began to kick in. 'Anyway, my father's not here so I don't need to bother.'

'You enjoy needling him, don't you?'

She refused to acknowledge the question and reached to pour herself another glass of wine.

'I suppose you think it's your duty as the resident black sheep of the family,' he added.

She sipped at her wine before finally responding.

'I don't have a lot of time for people who are too heavenly good to be of any earthly use.'

'Strong words from the daughter of a man who wants to be the next archbishop,' he put in.

'Look, don't get me wrong. I care about both of my parents but their beliefs are not mine, and I won't be forced to do or say anything I don't want to.'

'I'll have to remember that.'

'Yes, you will.'

She was glad when he went to the refrigerator once more to organise some food for them. She was on shaky ground with so much alcohol in her system, and she didn't trust herself not to start saying things she had no right saying to him or anyone.

'How about some smoked salmon quiche and salad?'

'Fine by me,' she said as he brought over the food and set it out on the scrubbed pine table in the centre of the room.

'We could eat in the dining room but it's probably warmer in here,' he said, holding out her chair.

She sat down, conscious of his large frame leaning over her. She could smell his aftershave, a spicy, heady concoction that she knew she'd always associate with him. She held her breath until he moved to take the chair opposite, his eyes meeting and holding hers.

'More wine?'

'Why not?'

'Why not, indeed?' He reached behind himself for the bottle and topped up her glass, leaving his own as it was.

She bent her head to the food in front of her and, picking up her knife and fork, began applying herself to the task of eating to avoid having to make conversation rather than any particularly pressing need for food.

Her appetite had waned hours ago when she'd joined him in front of the marriage celebrant, her stomach hollowing as she'd taken her place by his tall side, his broad shoulder touching hers as they both turned to face the front. The enormity of what she'd been about to do had struck her then more than at any other moment. As they'd signed the marriage certificate a few minutes later she'd truly felt as if she'd signed her life away. The sinking feeling in her stomach hadn't gone away even now, all these hours later. A great yawning emptiness, reminding her of all she wanted but could never have…

'You don't seem all that hungry,' Connor observed after a few minutes watching her shred her salad into tiny pieces, none of them quite making the distance to her pensive mouth.

Jasmine blinked and looked down at her plate.

'Oh.' She gave a cherry tomato a little push with her fork

and it rolled like a beach ball to the side of her plate. She put her knife and fork down and met his compelling gaze.

'I'm sorry. I had a big breakfast.'

He studied her for a long moment, his handsome head on one side, his dark hair ruffled, making her fingers twitch with the desire to thread themselves through the silky curls. She thrust her hands in her lap and forced herself to hold his gaze.

'Is there a telephone?' she asked. 'I need to ring the clinic to tell them how long I'll be away.'

'I've already done that.'

She felt herself tense in growing annoyance at the way he kept stepping over her personal boundaries. First, having his housekeeper pack her things and then calling the clinic.

'You had no right to do that.' The air crackled with her anger.

He held her look, his eyes so intent she was sure he could see right through her to the back of the chair where her trembling shoulders were pressed.

'I had every right to ensure you have a decent honeymoon period.'

'Decent?' The word came out as a harsh grunt of cynicism. 'There is absolutely nothing about any of this that is decent!' She got to her feet in agitation, tossing the napkin on to the table with a slash of her hand.

'Jasmine…' His tone was cautionary, which made her all the angrier.

'Don't you "Jasmine" me,' she shot back with a passable imitation of his deep intonation. She caught the tail end of his little smile of amusement and stamped her foot at him. 'I told you to stop laughing at me.'

He got to his feet in a single movement, his sudden increase of height making her shiver in apprehension. She couldn't read his expression accurately but thought it was somewhere between anger and frustration as he laid his napkin down with exaggerated precision even though his eyes never once left hers.

'I think you should take yourself off to bed,' he said in a tone one might have expected to hear when speaking to a small, over-tired child. 'You're beginning to sound distinctly shrewish.'

She gasped at his effrontery.

'And why wouldn't I be shrewish? You've dragged me to this God-forsaken gothic gargoyle-adorned disintegrating dosshouse just so you can inveigle your way into my underwear.'

His brows rose in mocking admiration at her wordy diatribe.

'They say alcohol loosens the tongue. In your case it's just off-loaded half the dictionary.'

She was beyond containing her rage. She moved from her chair, uncaring that the action toppled over the glasses, spilling wine everywhere. His glass rolled off the table and shattered at his feet, the sound of it breaking filling the flinty silence with an ominous edge.

This time she was in no doubt of his expression. He was angry, possibly more so than she'd ever seen him. His jaw was tight, the evening shadow on his jaw not able to disguise the flicker of a pulse at the side of his firm mouth, the shadows cast by the single light bulb overhead unable to conceal the glitter of reproach in his darkly hooded gaze.

'That was not a very nice thing to do,' he said after an interminable pause.

'I don't care,' she tossed back recklessly. 'You deserved it. I wish it had been red wine and stained your trousers.'

'If that had been red wine you'd be flat on your back by now with me staking the claim that I should have staked the moment we walked into this house.'

Her head reared back at the crudity of his statement. A host of disturbing images flooded her mind—images of his large body pinning her to the floor of the sitting room, the flickering flames from the fire nothing compared to the heat and fire of his touch on her fevered skin. She felt her innermost intimate muscles clench involuntarily at the thought of his hard length filling her, his milky fluid bursting from him at the peak of his pleasure…

'I must remember to make sure you never consume red wine in my presence.' She made an attempt to lighten the atmosphere.

He wasn't letting her off that easily.

'After you've cleaned that up I'll show you where we'll both be sleeping.' He stepped over the broken glass and, before she could open her mouth to tell him what to do with his arrogant command, he'd gone from the room, clipping the door shut behind him.

Jasmine stared at the mess on the floor. She refused to feel ashamed about her loss of control. He'd asked for it, damn him! Teasing her all the time, laughing at her behind those chocolate eyes, biding his time until he made the final swoop and made her his in every sense of the word.

She'd show him! She snatched at a dustpan and brush and shoved the broken fragments into the bin. She gathered the dishes and, after giving them a cursory scrape, left them in the sink. She'd be damned if she'd turn into his galley slave as well as his sex slave.

She stomped from the kitchen, intent on tracking him down in the big old house to inform him that even if there was only one bed left on the planet she was *not* going to share it with *him*.

He was in the main bedroom, a lovely room with large bay windows which in daylight afforded a beautiful view over Pelican Head. The old bed seemed to dominate the room, even though by any standards the room was commodious.

He turned as she flung open the door with a theatrical shove of her hand.

'I'm not sleeping with you in that bed.'

'I see.'

She hunted his face for a clue to what was going on behind

that impenetrable mask but his cool indifference gave nothing away.

'It's unthinkable,' she added.

'Quite.'

She opened and closed her fists by her sides.

'It's not that you're not very attractive…' She gnawed her bottom lip as she tried to back out of that very obvious compliment. 'What I mean is…I can't do it. I just can't!'

'I understand.'

She pressed her lips together tightly, not trusting herself to continue confessing rather more than she wanted to confess.

'I'll sleep on the sofa downstairs,' he offered gallantly.

She ran her tongue across the parchment of her lips.

'That's very…kind of you.'

'No trouble.' He picked up his things off the bed, a small shaving bag and his bathrobe, and left her in the middle of the room—alone.

She stared at the now closed door and frowned. She knew she shouldn't be feeling this gnawing sense of disappointment but, damn it, she did!

She turned around and sat heavily on the big bed, instantly sinking into the depths of the old mattress. A cloud of dust rose in the air and she sneezed.

'Some honeymoon,' she said under her breath, giving the springy mattress a punch with her fist. She sneezed again and her eyes began to water.

Damn him! She sprang to her feet and, kicking off her shoes, padded back downstairs to have it out with him.

She opened the sitting room door and pulled up short when she encountered him standing totally naked in front of the sofa preparing to settle down for the night.

'Did you want something?' he asked with an air of nonchalance she assumed came from being viewed naked by legions of women.

'I…' She swallowed and forced her eyes north of the border with considerable difficulty. 'No, I was just going to say…'

'Is the bed not comfortable?' he asked.

'No, it's...' She clutched at the lifeline as a drowning person did a float. 'Yes! That's why I came down here. I'm allergic to that bed.'

'Allergic?' His dark brows rose in twin question marks on his forehead.

'I...I sneezed.'

'That hardly constitutes an allergy.'

'Twice,' she added hastily. 'And my eyes are watering.'

'They look fine to me.'

She stomped across the floor and stood right in front of him and pointed to her itching eyes.

'See?' She blinked a couple of times. 'That's what I'd call an allergic reaction.'

She opened her eyes to see him studying her features, as if seeing them for the very first time.

'Nope.' He shook his head. 'I think you're overreacting.'

'Overreacting?' she gasped. 'I won't sleep a wink tonight because of you!'

'Ditto, so we're square at least.'

It took her a moment to understand his meaning and when she did she blushed to the roots of her hair.

She swung away but in her haste her bare toes caught in the ragged edge of the worn carpet and she felt herself falling.

He caught her and pulled her upright against him, her back pressing into the wall of his chest and stomach, and what was just below...

'You need to take a little more care, Jasmine,' he said, his voice a soft rumble along her liquefying spine. 'With all that alcohol on board you might find yourself doing things you might not normally do.'

She turned without thinking, still pressed far too close to him but beyond caring.

'I'm not drunk if that's what you're implying.'

'I didn't say you were.'

'You hinted at it.'

His expression was all innocence. 'I did no such thing.'

'You're laughing at me again,' she tried to growl at him but somehow her voice came out husky instead. 'I told you not to laugh at me.'

'Believe me, Jasmine—' his tone was wry '—I'm not laughing.'

She felt the unmistakable heat against her stomach where her body was pressed up against his. Her legs went to jelly and her stomach clenched as she saw his physical reaction to her reflected in the dark, deep pools of his eyes.

It was hard to say who moved first. Jasmine assumed it had been him, but later, reflection caused her to wonder if it had been her mouth that had pressed itself against the firm line of his.

All she knew was his mouth was back on hers, his tongue seeking entry, and she gave it willingly, softening against his hardness, unfolding all her tight barriers in his commanding male presence.

She could feel the nectar of her need pooling between her thighs. Her body ached to be filled, its pulse of blood reminding her of a need she could no longer ignore—no matter the consequences. She couldn't resist him any longer. She didn't see the point. Surely it was inevitable that they would finally end up in each other's arms, however short the interval. Once he discovered how unresponsive she was she knew he'd be back off to bachelordom without a backward glance.

He pressed her to the floor with a gentleness that surprised her considering the highly aroused state of his body. He took his time, peeling away her dress, deftly removing her plain bra, her breasts spilling into his waiting warm hands.

She felt his mouth take each nipple in turn, subjecting them to an exploration of his teeth and tongue until she was writhing with the sensations gathering inside her.

He slid down her body and she sucked in her breath as his long fingers began sliding away her panties, the glide of fabric down her thigh a delicious torture in her state of heightened awareness. She felt his warm breath on her intimately, and instantly tensed.

He placed a palm on the flat plane of her belly and its heat seemed to seep through to the very core of her, melting her momentary resistance.

'Trust me, Jasmine.' He breathed the words against her tender flesh.

She shut her eyes and let herself feel as he explored her pulsing need, taking his time acquainting himself with her delicate detail.

She drew in a ragged breath as he found what he was looking for.

'Oh!' She couldn't stop the gasp in time. She clutched at his dark curls and held on as the spasm tightened her legs as it flew along her veins like a furious fire in search of fuel.

She clamped down on her lips to stop the cries coming out but it was no good. Her body was taking her on a journey she was unprepared for; there was nothing she could do to stop it.

He slid back up to anchor himself up on his elbows either side of her still gasping form. She felt his throbbing maleness so close she wanted to grasp at him but when she reached out a tentative hand his fingers closed over her arm, stalling her mission.

'I have to protect you,' he said and, rolling away, dug his fingers into his shaving bag by the sofa and retrieved a tiny foil packet. He took the edge of it in his straight white teeth and tore it, spitting the edge of it out of one side of his mouth in a bone-meltingly male fashion that made her almost mindless with lust.

She watched as he applied the protection with practised ease but this time she was beyond caring how many women had gone before. All she knew was that she was the one beneath his hard body now, and it was her desire he would be fulfilling.

He pressed her back down and gently slid into her warm

feminine cocoon with a deep groan that surprised her. Somehow she'd imagined someone with his depth of experience would find her body very humdrum but he appeared to be deeply moved by the feel of her muscles tightening around him.

'Am I hurting you?' His voice was just a whisper against her mouth.

'No,' she breathed back against his lips.

He increased his pace just a notch, gently at first; then as she welcomed him with increasing confidence he drove a fraction harder and deeper. She could hardly believe what she was feeling; it was so different from her first time. That time she had been embarrassed at her ineptness at insufficiently arousing a young man who on record had bedded most of her year as well as a considerable portion of the year above. This was nothing like it. Connor had drawn from her a response she hadn't known she'd been capable of. Great waves of feeling washed over her, rolling her over and over in their intensity. She heard her keening cries as he took her once more to the pinnacle with every deep surge of his body in hers. She went willingly, with abandon, with relish, with joy.

She was still coming back down to earth when his release sounded in her ear in a deep groan of expelled breath. She listened to the sounds of his pleasure—his faster than normal breathing, the tenseness of his muscles and then the swift descent into relaxation afterwards, his large body collapsing against hers, spent in pleasure.

She wasn't game enough to move. She hardly breathed in case she disturbed the moment, frightened he would spoil it by mocking her inexperience, shaming her the way she'd been shamed before.

Sudden doubt assailed her.

Connor felt her tense beneath him. He rolled off and, leaning on one elbow, surveyed the complex emotions flickering over her features as he slowly trailed an idle finger down between her breasts.

He heard her swift intake of breath as his finger came up to circle one rosy nipple.

'You like that?' His eyes burned down into hers.

She didn't respond in words but his question had been answered all the same. He moved to the other breast and repeated the movement, watching as she struggled to disguise her reaction to him.

She intrigued him. The way she fought him at every turn, her defiance the biggest turn on he'd ever experienced. He'd wanted her from the first moment he'd seen her on the day of his stepbrother's engagement party. She'd glared at him from time to time, which had only served to inflame him even more. And now he had her in his arms where he wanted her to stay—permanently. He couldn't help smiling at how much he'd changed. Who would recognise the play hard playboy now?

'I need the bathroom.' The prosaic tone of Jasmine's voice was a little unnerving under the circumstances of their recent intimacy but he knew she was keen to put some distance between them.

'Be my guest.' He released her from his light hold, watching her as she fought with herself about whether to get up and reveal her nakedness to him as she left the room.

He heard her breath of resignation as she got to her feet and, snatching up her discarded dress, clutched it to her chest.

What did one say in this sort of situation, Jasmine wondered? Thank you for the lesson in sensuality. I'm sure it will come in very handy in the future?

She bit her lip.

Connor got to his feet and reached for his bathrobe, which was draped across the back of the sofa.

'Here.' He handed it to her. 'It's cold in the bathroom. You'd better wear this.'

She could smell his body's exclusive scent as she wrapped herself in his robe. The soft folds of fabric almost covered her, consuming her just as he had done a few minutes ago.

She felt a combination of gratitude at his sensitivity and shame at herself for needing it so badly. What was wrong with her? Why couldn't she just enjoy the moment for what it was—a pleasant interlude of passion and unrestrained lust? Why ask for anything else? What more could he give other than the heat of his body and the temporary comfort of his arms?

She stepped over his long, outstretched legs and left the room, but she felt his dark eyes on her all the way to the door and even when she closed it softly behind her.

CHAPTER EIGHT

JASMINE took her time in the bathroom. The ancient plumbing surprised her in allowing her to shower in relative comfort although, as Connor had warned, the old bathroom was a little cold.

She stared at her reflection in the speckled mirror, hardly recognising herself. Her eyes were different, pupils wide and extended as if she'd just woken up from a very long sleep. Her mouth was still slightly swollen from Connor's deep kisses, and when she pressed her thighs together she could feel the intimate place where he'd so recently been.

It felt strange to feel him on her skin. She could smell his presence even after her shower. It felt as if he'd indelibly marked her as his. She was sure no one else could ever make her feel the way he did. The only trouble was, she was just one of many to him. There was no future in a relationship that had come about the way theirs had.

She'd fought her feelings for him from the moment she'd met him; it was as if she'd innately sensed he was danger personified. But it hadn't done her any good because, in spite of her determination to keep him at arm's length, her heart had already capitulated to his disarming version of humour and charm. A deadly concoction that she was fiercely tempted to keep sipping for as long as she possibly could...

When she went back to the sitting room he had stoked the fire and was standing before its warm glow, the strong flanks of his muscled thighs cast in gold. He looked over his shoulder at her as she came in, a small smile lurking about the corners of his mouth.

He was still naked, she noted, with a sweep of her gaze

113

that this time lingered a little more than she'd allowed previously.

'Pleased to see me?' It was her first attempt at flirting with him and it gave her a heady feeling.

His eyes meshed with hers. 'What do you think?'

Her eyes lowered and she felt a trickle of excitement pool in her stomach at his extended arousal.

'On the evidence at hand I'd say that was a yes.'

He moved towards her. Her breath locked in her throat as he reached out a hand and captured a strand of long chestnut hair. He coiled it around his finger again and again until she could feel herself being pulled ever so gently and inexorably closer and closer into the waiting heat of his body.

'It's a very definite yes,' he said just above her mouth.

His mouth came down to hers and time ceased to exist once more. He sucked on her bottom lip, drawing it into the heat of his mouth. His slow-moving tongue unfolded and dipped into the recesses of her mouth, leaving her breathless with mindless need.

She pressed against him with female instinct, the softness of her body seeking the all conquering male strength of his. He lowered her to the floor and held her down with the weight of his frame, his arrant maleness slipping between her thighs like an arrow from a quiver. She gasped at his sudden entry, caught up in the wave of his urgent desire, wondering why it had taken until this very moment to realise she loved him. But then how could she not? His gentleness had been her undoing; he'd unravelled her just like a strand of yarn from a tightly wound ball. Even if she tried she knew she'd never be able to tighten her defences again. He'd slipped through and there was no going back.

She didn't want to remind herself of the temporary arrangement of their marriage, a marriage conducted solely to keep the baying hounds of the press and the more repressed members of both their families off their backs. It couldn't last, she knew that, but for the first time in her life she wanted to live in the moment only, take a risk, live out a dream, even though it would very likely end in a nightmare of hurt and rejection.

Connor felt the increasing urgency of her mouth and hands as she explored him, her small fingers running over the muscles of his back and shoulders, lingering in his hair, sending shivers of need up along his spine. He was losing control but it didn't matter as she was with him all the way, her body rising to greet his every deepening thrust.

There wasn't time for thinking; this was all about feeling and finding the fulfilment they both craved. He felt her slip over the edge, her slender body tightening around him, drawing him in and sucking on his heat as if within it was the breath which she needed to breathe.

It was an almost savage release for him, a violent burst of feeling that filled his head with a kaleidoscope of fragmenting colours cascading around his brain. Her ragged breathing filled his ears, her chest rising and falling in time with his, her breasts crushed between his pectoral muscles, their rounded mounds spilling upwards as if seeking his mouth.

Jasmine opened her eyes and found him looking at her, his body still encased in hers but relaxed now.

'You have such beautiful breasts,' he said.

She didn't know what to say. Thank you seemed so formal and polite, especially after the intimacy they'd just shared.

'Why the act?' he asked when she didn't speak.

'Act?' She looked at him blankly.

He coiled a strand of her hair around his finger once more, leaving her no choice but to hold his look.

'The look-at-me-I'm-an-outrageous-tart act.' A little smile accompanied his words.

She swallowed. 'You could tell?'

He nodded.

'Was I...so bad?' Doubt seeped into her tone, her cheeks already growing hot at the thought of her failure to please him.

His mouth lifted in a sexy smile.

'You ask *that* after what we just shared?'

She pressed her lips together and tasted him.

'I...I'm not an expert on these situations,' she said. 'As you no doubt can tell.'

'You're a very sexy young woman, Jasmine.' His pupils widened as his gaze swept over her full breasts again. 'You make me lose control. No one has done that in years.'

'I'm sorry.'

He threw back his head and laughed and she felt it in her stomach as his abdomen rippled along hers.

'You're also one of the most amusing women I've ever met,' he added, still smiling down at her. 'And that's the biggest turn-on in the world.'

'It is?' She sneaked her tongue out to moisten the dryness of her lips. He followed the movement with his eyes, his own mouth coming closer and closer until it was barely a millimetre away.

'You bet it is,' he said and covered her mouth with his.

It was a long and languorous coupling, slow and sensuous, bringing Jasmine bit by bit towards a higher level of physical consciousness. Her body seemed to be melting in the heat and passion of his, her softness swallowed by his hardness. She felt a sort of completeness in his arms that went further than simply the appeasement of fleshly desires.

When the storm of passion had receded, Connor kissed the tip of her nose before getting to his feet with the sort of agility she privately envied. Her body felt as if someone had loosened all its joints, leaving her boneless, too relaxed to move.

She watched him as he scooped up the cushions off the sofa and laid them on the floor next to her in front of the glowing fire. He picked up the throw rug and, once she was settled on the cushions, gathered it around them both. She felt cocooned in sensual warmth, the scent of their spent desire filling the air around them.

They lay in a silence broken only by the occasional spitting of a log as it released some sap into the fire. Jasmine had never realised before how deeply erotic a fire could be—the heat of glowing embers, the leap of flames as more fuel was laid down, the hiss and spit of released juices as the wood was consumed.

She felt Connor shift his arm from under her neck, turning slightly so he could look at her in the incandescent glow of the fire.

'Where are you in your cycle?'

The question seemed to come from nowhere and it took her a while to grasp the context.

'I'm due any time,' she found herself saying.

His relief was almost palpable.

'I didn't wear a condom after the first time, sorry.' A brief frown of contrition flicked across his forehead. 'I got carried away and put you at risk.'

'I'll be fine,' she said, hoping it was true.

'I don't have any nasty diseases, if that's what's bothering you,' he added when he saw her frown forming.

'The thought never crossed my mind.'

He traced the line of her mouth with one lazy finger.

'You should mind,' he said. 'Encounters like this could change your life in a second.'

She wanted to tell him it had changed her life permanently, but bit back the words.

'I'm sure I'll live to tell the tale.'

He hunted her face for a few moments, as if he could see behind her miserable attempt at humour and was going to call her to account. But after a while he simply dropped another swift kiss on to the tip of her nose and slid back down beside her, gathering her back into his warm embrace.

'Let's get some sleep.' His voice was a soft burr in her ear.

She shut her eyes and concentrated on listening to the sound of the fire. After a few minutes Connor's even breathing informed her he had drifted off to sleep. She laid her head on his chest and breathed in the scent of his skin and wondered if he'd still be there in her arms in the morning.

* * *

Jasmine woke up alone but she could hear the sounds of Connor moving about the house. She rolled on to her other side and listened to the chorus of birds outside the bay windows, their cheery song failing to lift her spirits at all.

She dragged herself from the warmth of the makeshift bed, her body protesting inside and out at the movement. She hunted for some clothes but only found Connor's bathrobe. She slipped her arms through the sleeves and, stepping over the disarray of the sofa cushions, made her way to the bathroom.

Her mood hadn't lifted even after her shower. With the morning had come the recriminations from her behaviour the night before. She scowled at herself in the steamed up mirror, hating herself for having capitulated so readily. A couple of glasses of wine and she was anybody's—and not just anybody's, but Connor Harrowsmith's, one of the biggest playboys of all time. It didn't salve her conscience one iota to remind herself she was in love with him and had every right to express that physically. Somehow it made it so much worse. It wasn't as if she could come right out and say, 'By the way, I really love you in spite of the bizarre circumstances surrounding our marriage'. She'd look a fool and no doubt his response would be to laugh or, even worse, smile one of those mocking smiles.

She tossed her towel to the floor on top of Connor's with a spurt of defiance. Let him pick them up, she wasn't going to be running around after him like some downtrodden housewife while he went off and charmed the birds from the trees, the office, nightclub or wherever he found his latest conquests.

She found him in the back garden, hanging out the bed linen from the master bedroom she'd refused to sleep in. He turned to look her way, even though she was absolutely sure she'd made no sound. She wondered if he had a sixth sense where she was concerned, or whether he could read her mind.

'How are you feeling?' he asked, ducking under the clothes line.

'I'm sore,' she said bluntly, forcing herself to look him in the eyes.

His small smile had a trace of apology about it.

'If you had been straight with me about your level of experience perhaps I would've compensated a little more.'

'I wasn't exactly a virgin.'

'No, perhaps not technically, but you're hardly a seasoned tart though, are you?'

'I am now.'

He frowned heavily. 'What's that supposed to mean?'

She scowled at him darkly. 'What number am I on your bedpost, Connor? Do you keep a running record?'

He stood looking at her assessingly, his continued silence intimidating her into further reckless speech.

'Or maybe you have a little black book in which you write all the details, such as how enjoyable it was for you, whether you'd like to continue the relationship or not, or whether she was fat or thin or had big boobs or—'

'If this attack is expressly aimed at alleviating some of your own guilt over your responses to me, then stop right now.'

His terse words brought her head up straight.

'My guilt?' she threw at him incredulously. 'What about yours?'

'I did nothing you didn't want me to do.'

'Yes, you did. I told you I didn't want to sleep with you and you took advantage of my...of the fact that I'd had a couple of drinks and wasn't thinking clearly.'

His jaw tightened, which should have warned her to drop it right there, but her fighting spirit and her pride had already combined forces.

'I despise men like you; your selfishness knows no bounds. It's all about getting laid at whatever cost, even marriage in your case.'

'I think you've said quite enough, Jasmine.' His tone was steely. 'I can see you're having second thoughts about last night but don't make me your scapegoat. You came to me quite willingly and I did what any normal man would do under the circumstances.'

'I want to go home right now!' she said. 'I don't want to stay another minute here with you.'

'Don't be so melodramatic.' His tone was impatient. 'If we go back to the city after less than twenty-four hours it will cause the sort of speculation neither of us need right now.'

'I'd rather face the press than spend another night in your arms.'

'We both know that isn't true.' His dark eyes held hers challengingly, daring her to contradict him.

She glared back at him rebelliously.

'Why did you bring me here? Why not a decent hotel instead of this rat-infested place?'

'I got rid of the rats last week and, as for the cobwebs, I was going to do that this afternoon.'

Jasmine gaped at him speechlessly.

'I know it's not exactly The Ritz, but with a little attention it could be made very comfortable. Anyway, no one but us knows about this place so, for a few days at least, we're safe,' he continued calmly.

She found her tongue at last. 'There were *rats* here last week?' She couldn't help a tiny shudder and a furtive glance around her feet.

'Not many.'

'H…how many?' her eyes were wide with fear.

'You don't like rats?'

'Give me a snake any day.' She gave another shudder.

Connor smiled and picked up the clothes basket.

'Come on, let's have some breakfast before we go down to the beach.'

Jasmine found herself following him into the house despite her earlier determination to avoid him at all costs. Her eyes darted about the kitchen as he filled the kettle with water, fully expecting tiny black eyes to be staring from between the gaps in the skirting boards, waiting for their chance to flash past under her feet.

Connor handed her a cup but it slipped from her grasp and landed at his feet in a myriad of pieces.

He gave her a wry look.

'You're really on edge, aren't you?'

'I'm fine.' She paid no attention to his comment as she went to get the dustpan and broom she'd used the night before.

It was unfortunate she hadn't put it away properly for when she opened the broom cupboard door the small brush with its grey-black bristles dropped near her foot.

Her scream filled every corner of the room. Connor swung around to find her on the table, her face a ghostly white, her limbs trembling like the autumn leaves outside.

'Hey there, sweetheart.' His tone was instantly placating as he reached up a hand to her. 'Did the big bad old brush give you a terrible fright?'

She glowered down at him, ignoring his hand.

'Don't you dare laugh at me, just don't you dare.'

He held up his hands in a gesture of complete innocence.

'Now would I do that?'

'Yes, you would.'

He gave a mock pout.

'I'm hurt, crushed in fact, that you think so poorly of me.'

She clambered down from the table and stood fuming in front of him.

'You are one of the most annoying men I've ever had the misfortune to meet, do you know that?'

He gave her a sweeping bow.

'At your service, ma'am.'

She flung herself away and stomped out of the kitchen without a backward glance, all her appetite for breakfast completely gone.

She found her clothes in the upstairs bedroom, where she saw Connor had stripped the bed and opened all the windows to air the room. She dressed in track pants and top, relieved that she didn't sneeze once. Making her way back downstairs, she left the house through a side door so she didn't run into him.

Only when she was finally on the beach did she start to relax enough to gather her thoughts. She walked along the water's edge, the swell hissing and retreating at her feet, the crunch of shells like percussion in her ears. Two gulls soared above her head and then, catching an up-draught of air, flew off to the cliff face once more.

The slight breeze was chilly but refreshing as she walked towards the first group of rock pools about two kilometres away in the distance. When she got there she bent down to inspect the contents of the biggest pools, dangling her fingers in the slightly warmer water where the morning sun had lingered. Two purple anemones, their white spines close to their round bodies, lay undisturbed amongst the bright green seaweed.

She sat on the bump of a rock and stared out to sea. The rolling waves were soothing as they crashed against the shore, every fifth or sixth one spilling over the rock pools before draining away once more.

It was a noisy peace. The harsh cries of gulls and the roar of the sea, combined with the deepening breathing of the wind, made her sigh with tentative pleasure. Her paradise was not the same with Connor there to invade her sense of peace. He made her feel edgy and on guard, especially now as he'd broken down another barrier to brand her as his.

She knew she was being unreasonable towards him, blaming him for what after all was her own fault. She'd practically thrown herself at him, subconsciously at least, when she'd gone to have it out with him over the sleeping arrangements. A tiny part of her mind had to admit the risks she'd been taking in going back to confront him, but she'd ignored those warnings to rush headlong into a situation that would in the end only hurt her.

He was invincible. His heart was whole and untouched while hers was now his and very likely to be destroyed.

She took shelter from the wind in a sea cave she'd found on one of her walks previously. It was tucked into the cliff face, its steep access making it almost invisible from the beach.

She sat on the rocky ledge and listened to the roar of the sea below, lifting her face every now and again to catch the fine mist of sea spray in the air. She brushed at her eyes once or twice, refusing to give in to the desire to cry. She hadn't cried in years and had no intention of resurrecting the habit, no matter how vulnerable Connor made her feel.

The wind had died down when she left the cave a long time later. She retraced her steps along the sand, her head down, concentrating on placing one foot in front of the other in the steps she'd trod earlier, not wanting to disturb the long stretch of sand any more than she had. She managed to get to the first rock pool without a step out of place but when she came off the rocks to retrace her earlier footsteps she saw that her small ones had been crushed by a much larger foot.

She spun around and saw the culprit bending down over one of the rock pools to her right. She hadn't seen him before as her head had been down, retracing her steps, but she knew before he stood up to his full height it was Connor.

She considered pretending she hadn't seen him but before she could escape he turned and faced her. She waited until he skirted around the rock pools to get to her, his steps unhurried, but she could tell from the tight look about his mouth he was annoyed with her.

She straightened her spine as he closed the distance.

'You've been gone over three hours.' His tone was curt.

'So?'

'So you should tell me where you're going.'

'Why should I?'

He clenched his teeth. 'Because it's polite to tell people where you're going, that's why.'

'It's no one's business where I go.'

'As much as it pains me to disagree with you, I'm afraid it is very much my business.'

'You take your responsibilities as a husband a little too far, as I told you earlier.' Sarcasm laced her tone.

His eyes ran over her, taking in her wind-blown hair and reddened eyes.

'Have you been crying?' he asked, his tone gentled.

'Of course not.' She spun away to walk back to the cliff path. 'I got sand in my eyes. It was windy earlier.'

He seemed satisfied with her answer and adjusted his stride to hers as they traversed the rest of the beach to the path.

'You must be starving,' he said after a few minutes. 'You didn't have breakfast and its way past lunch.'

'It won't hurt me; I need to lose some weight anyway.'

'As it is, you look as if a gust of wind would blow you over,' he observed.

'I'm sure you're used to the very best in female figures,' she said with a trace of bitterness. 'Sorry to disappoint you.'

'You'd be surprised.'

'I'm sure.'

He gave her a sideways smile.

'If I didn't know you better I'd say you were just a tiny bit jealous.'

She stopped at the base of the cliff path and faced him.

'Sorry to disappoint you, but I don't feel anything towards you except dislike.'

'That's not the message I was getting last night.'

'I was not myself last night.'

'Ah yes, last night was an aberration never to be repeated, is that right?'

'Yes, that's exactly right.'

He gestured for her to precede him on the cliff path. 'You go first; I'll be here in case you fall.'

'You go first,' she insisted. 'I'm not going to fall.'

He shrugged his shoulders and leapt up the path like a

mountain goat, leaving her to clamber up by herself a little more circumspectly. He was waiting for her at the top, his expression showing signs of amusement as she joined him.

'What's so funny?' she asked irritably.

'You are.'

'Why?'

'Because you hide behind anger to cover other more dangerous emotions.'

She made to brush past him. 'I don't know what you're talking about.'

His arm caught hers on the way past and he turned her to face him. She schooled her features into resentful defiance but she knew the sheen of fresh tears was in her eyes.

'Yes, you do,' he said. 'Whenever anyone gets within touching distance you put up a great wall of anger to warn them off. That's why you're so cross with me about last night because you let your guard slip, but it's not really me you're angry with, is it, Jasmine?'

She averted her gaze and aimed it at a point to the left of his broad shoulder.

'Strange as it may seem, I am actually angry with you. I suppose it's a kind of novelty for you to have a woman tell you that but it's true.'

'Look me in the eyes and say that,' he challenged her.

She locked eyes with his. 'I'm angry with you, Connor.'

Somehow the way she said his name took away from the conviction of her other words; it came out huskily, like a caress, instead of sharply and implacably as she'd intended.

His wry smile was back in place.

'I like you being angry with me,' he said.

She blinked up at him in confusion. 'Why?'

'Because it shows you feel something towards me.'

'I don't feel—'

His fingers gently pinched her two lips together, halting her speech.

'Don't,' he said as softly as the breeze moving through her

hair. 'You keep on being angry with me. In fact, you should be furious with me, speechless with rage.'

He let go of her lips in time for her to ask somewhat ironically, 'Why?'

He bent his mouth to hers and kissed her deeply before responding.

'Is that a good enough reason?'

She opened and closed her throbbing mouth, uncertain of how to respond.

'I'll take that as a yes, then,' he said and, before she could reply, he disappeared along the path, leaving her to stand staring at the space he'd vacated.

CHAPTER NINE

JASMINE took the long way back to the old house.

She knew it was being cowardly but she couldn't help thinking that Connor had manipulated her into confessing something she hadn't wanted to confess. She replayed the conversation in her head and had to concede that he was a master at playing conversational games, cutting her off at every pass, anticipating her every move as if he were able to see through the tangle of her thoughts.

She entered the house the same way she'd exited it and, listening out for sounds of his presence, made her way cautiously to the kitchen for something to ease the gnaw of hunger in her stomach.

She'd not long finished a tomato sandwich when he came in, brandishing a long-handled broom.

'I've finished the cobwebs but I was wondering if you'd give me a hand in the study.'

She looked at him warily.

'Doing what?'

'I promise you—no rats, spiders or snakes, just a whole heap of books.'

'Books?'

He nodded.

'I'm not a classics fan but even I can see value in some of those titles. Some of them look like they might be first editions.'

He'd won her without a fight. Books were her passion and old ones in particular.

'All right.' She got to her feet, noting the tiny gleam of victory in his dark eyes. She felt as if she'd been cleverly manipulated again but for the life of her couldn't imagine what he'd be up to this time.

She followed him down the dark hall and tried not to let her eyes wander to the cracks in the skirting boards nor flinch at the creak of old floorboards.

The study smelt musty but she managed to suppress her reactive sneeze long enough to look around.

The shelves along three walls were floor to ceiling and each of them was lined with books. A leather-top desk was in front of the window and the maroon velvet curtains were heavily faded with tiny holes in the aged fabric letting pinholes of sunlight through. Dust motes rose in the air each time either of them moved but Jasmine hardly noticed. Her attention was on the gold-embossed spines of the books on the shelves before her at eye level, some of the higher ones looking even more impressive.

She sucked in a breath of excitement.

'This is amazing.' Her eyes shone as she reached out and touched a first edition of a children's book from the turn of the last century.

She turned to face him.

'Some of these books are priceless, do you realise that?'

He studied the excitement on her face for a long moment as if committing it to memory.

'I'm sure one or two will prove to be so.'

She would have frowned at his strange reply but the books were all she could think about at present. She turned back and, with fingers almost reverent, reached out and touched the spines at her level.

'I wish I'd known these books were here all this time.'

'Why?' Connor's voice sounded from somewhere behind her.

She didn't turn around but kept looking at the titles in front of her.

'I love old books. I love the smell of the pages and the thought of generations of people reading the same words time and time again.' She turned to frown at him. 'But why didn't the previous owner take them when they left?'

'I'm not sure,' he answered as he made his way to the door. 'I'll leave you to have a play while I make some inroads on dinner.'

She turned back to look at him.

'You don't mind if I stay here a while?'

He shook his head. 'Go right ahead. The closest I get to reading is the sports page in *The Herald*,' he confessed with a wry grin.

Of course she didn't believe him. How else would he have known the value of the books he'd led her to? But he closed the door before she could respond and she was left alone with a crowd of aged titles and a host of memories as she reached for the book nearest her.

He found her curled up on the cracked chesterfield an hour and a half later, her chestnut head buried in an early edition of Constance Mackness's *Di-Double-Di*.

'Good book?'

She looked up and smiled; the first genuine smile he'd seen on her beautiful face.

'Yes, I love this old book.'

He sat on the sofa beside her and peered over her shoulder at the book she had in her lap.

'What's it about?'

She closed the book, suddenly feeling embarrassed.

'Go on,' he urged. 'Tell me.'

'It's about two girls at boarding school who find a gap in the fence through to an adjoining property.'

'A girls' own adventure?' he guessed.

'Yes, you could call it that.'

'Happy ending?'

She nodded. 'Very happy.'

His eyes held hers for a fraction longer than necessary.

'Dinner is just about ready, if you're hungry.'

She gave him a guilty glance. 'I should be helping you with the cooking.'

'No problem. I enjoy it really; my housekeeper, Maria, has taught me a thing or two over the years.' He got to his feet and stretched.

Jasmine's eyes were instantly drawn to the ridged muscles of his abdomen that his close-fitting T-shirt revealed. His body was magnificent in every way possible—toned, tanned, taut, tall and devastatingly handsome, his firm mouth with its fuller bottom lip promising mind-blowing passion…

She tore her eyes away and got to her feet, barely registering the soft thud of the book as it slid to the floor at her feet.

'Connor, I…'

'Yes?' His tall body stood motionless, his eyes dark mysterious pools of some indefinable emotion as he looked down at her.

The intensity of his gaze made her hesitate. She caught her bottom lip between her teeth momentarily.

'What did you want to tell me, Jasmine?' he probed gently.

At the last minute she decided she couldn't do it. She'd wanted to tell him of her shifting feelings about him but when push came to shove the words just wouldn't come. She just couldn't allow herself to beg for a few crumbs of affection when what she really wanted was the whole package. She wanted him to love her. She wanted him to feel the same stomach-jerking pangs she felt every time she looked at him.

She stared at him blankly for a long minute before bending to pick up the book from the floor.

'Nothing.' She dusted off its fragile cover with a gentle brush of her hand. 'It was nothing important.'

Connor didn't press her, which made her feel grateful at a time when she wanted to distance herself in every way possible. He made her feel vulnerable and exposed as she wasn't used to someone being close enough to see through the mask she wore to cover her inner loneliness.

He held the door for her and she slipped past him with her

head down, not stopping until she came to the kitchen, conscious of his heavy tread behind her every step of the way.

Connor suggested they eat in the dining room, where he'd laid two places on one end of the long table. Jasmine took her seat as he dished up the veal and tomato casserole he'd prepared earlier, the deft movements of his hands reminding her all over again of what it felt like to have those hands on her, exploring her intimate contours, drawing from her a response she could still feel in her innermost body...

'Would you like some wine?' He poised the bottle near her glass.

Her eyes connected with his, her face instantly heating when she recalled how the wine had made her act so out of character the evening before.

'I think I'll give it a miss, if you don't mind,' she answered after the tiniest pause.

'Shame.' He filled his own glass and she was left to speculate on what exactly he meant by that one word delivered so dryly.

'This is very good,' she said after tasting the meal.

'Thank you.' He picked up his glass and took a sip.

Jasmine ate the meal in front of her more for something to do other than feast her eyes on his features all the time like some sort of lovesick schoolgirl. She took her time over every mouthful, stringing out the process so as to avoid making conversation.

Connor had finished his meal and, sipping his wine, watched her as she cut the last few morsels into the tiniest pieces, chewing them slowly, almost exaggeratedly.

He put his glass down and, leaning his elbows on the table in front of him, gave her a knowing smile.

'You find my company disturbing, don't you?'

She hoped her expression was suitably guileless as she looked across at him.

'Not at all.'

He raised a brow as he reached for his wine once more.

'What is it that threatens you the most?' he asked after a little pause.

She put her knife and fork down and dabbed at the corners of her mouth with her napkin to stall her reply.

'I don't find you threatening. I find you annoying.'

'Why?'

'Because you push me too far.'

'In what way?'

'In every way.'

'Be more specific.' He leant back in his chair, one arm slung casually over the back.

Jasmine pursed her lips before responding.

'You don't respect my personal space, for one thing.'

'You mean I come too close?'

'Far too close.'

'What else?'

'You don't take no for an answer.'

'I take it if I see it,' he said.

'What do you mean by that?' she asked.

He ran a finger around the lip of his glass, his eyes never once leaving hers.

'You might say no with your mouth but your body says yes every time.'

'That's not true.'

'What about last night?'

'What about it?'

'You wanted me as much as I wanted you. You spent most of the day saying no but when it came down to the crunch your body decided for you.'

'Last night was a mistake,' she said quickly, her colour high.

'It probably appeases your sense of propriety to see it that way, but I prefer to see it as two people who have a chemistry thing happening which they responded to instinctively.'

'You make it sound as if we had no choice in the matter.'

'We didn't,' he said. 'What happened was meant to happen.'

'Only because you were determined to make it happen.'

'Not at all,' he protested. 'I wasn't going to push you into something you weren't ready to do. I waited until you made the first move.'

'Define the first move.' Her tone was cynical. 'What did I do? Look at you for more than fifteen seconds or something?'

He smiled. 'You really won't admit it, will you?'

'Admit what?' She scowled at him.

'That you wanted me.'

'I did not want you. You took advantage of the situation.'

He picked up his glass and took a contemplative sip.

'You're not being honest with me or yourself. Why is it so hard for you to admit what you actually feel?'

'Damn it, Connor!' she almost shouted at him. 'You make me feel things I don't want to feel!'

'Like what?'

'Nothing.' She bit her lip. 'I feel nothing.'

'Tell me what you feel, Jasmine.'

Her fingers around her glass tightened agitatedly.

'I…I feel like…like someone else.'

'When you're with me?'

She nodded. 'I'm usually so in control, so neat, so tidy, everything in its place, you know?'

He nodded.

'But when I'm with you I feel…I feel…' She paused, searching for the right words.

'What do you feel, Jasmine?'

'I feel…out of control,' she confessed at last, lifting her eyes to his.

'Control is important to you, isn't it?' he asked.

She toyed with her glass distractedly.

'I don't like unpredictability. I like to know what's going on so I can be prepared. I don't feel like that around you. I don't know what's going on and I don't know how to prepare myself.'

'You don't need to prepare yourself at all,' he said gently. 'Just be yourself.'

'I don't know how to be myself any more.'

'Because of what happened with Roy Holden?'

She lifted her eyes to his briefly.

'That… And other things.'

'What other things?'

She lowered her gaze. 'Things I don't want to talk about.'

She bit her lip, trying not to give in to the threatening tears. She felt his hand reach out to touch her on her arm, the warmth of his palm seeping through her cold, stiff flesh, making it suddenly come alive with the pulse of blood. She lifted her gaze to find him looking at her, his expression serious but encouraging.

'Why don't you go and relax in the sitting room while I clear up here? I'll bring in some coffee shortly.'

She gave him a grateful half-smile and left the table, glad of an opportunity to gather her crumbling demeanour away from his all-seeing eyes.

Connor had laid a fire earlier and it was crackling merrily as she went into the room, its golden glow welcoming in spite of the aged furnishings and décor.

She deliberately avoided thinking about what the room had witnessed the night before and sat on the sofa and leafed through an old *National Geographic* magazine while she waited for him to join her.

He came in a few minutes later with freshly brewed coffee and two mugs on a tray, setting them down in front of her on the old coffee table.

'How do you have it?' he asked.

'Straight black,' she answered and took the mug from him, cradling her cold fingers around its warmth.

She sipped the hot liquid and watched as he stirred two

teaspoons of sugar in his own along with a generous splash of milk. He caught her eyes on him and gave a rueful smile.

'I know it's bad for the teeth, but so far so good.'

She couldn't argue with him over that; his straight, even teeth were the whitest she'd ever seen.

Connor allowed a little silence to settle between them. He sat back and drank his coffee, his eyes on the fire in the fireplace, his long legs stretched out before him, his feet crossed at the ankles.

Jasmine was sitting within touching distance and just knowing she could reach out with her fingers and stroke her hand along his firm thigh suddenly made it all the more tempting to do so.

She didn't know what was wrong with her. She'd been determined that the physical intimacy they'd shared was not to be repeated, for several reasons. Firstly she didn't want to complicate things between them, and secondly she wanted to be able to walk away with her pride intact when the time came. She couldn't imagine him staying married to anyone very long, least of all to her.

She sat on her hands to stop them from betraying her, but her movement caused him to look at her which somehow made things a whole lot worse. His dark eyes bored into her grey-blue ones, pinning her to the spot.

She ran her tongue over her dry lips in a nervous action that shifted his gaze to the fullness of her mouth. His face was shadowed with a day's growth of beard and she wanted to rasp her fingertips across the lean jaw, linger beside his mouth where his skin creased slightly whenever he smiled his bone-melting smile. She wanted to trace the fullness of his lower lip, run her fingertip down the length of his patrician nose and back up to his dark eyes, those eyes that sent shivers of anticipation down her spine each and every time they rested on her.

Her eyelids fluttered closed as his head came towards her,

her shoulders relaxing as his mouth pressed hers once in a kiss as soft as the brush of a feather.

He leant back and she opened her eyes, giving his features a searching look.

He tucked a wayward strand of her hair behind one of her ears, the tiny movement sending an arc of feeling straight to the hollowness of her belly.

She wanted him to kiss her again, properly. She wondered he didn't see it in her eyes and the slight lean of her body towards him.

'Connor…' She breathed his name.

His hand cupped the side of her face, holding her gaze to his.

'Jasmine, I want you right now.'

'I know.' The thought thrilled her even as it terrified her.

He got to his feet and, taking her hand, pulled her up to stand before him. She could feel the warmth of his body emanating towards her, drawing her to him like a moth to a flame. She knew ultimately she was going to get hurt but she couldn't seem to help herself. She needed him, wanted him and to hell with the consequences—she was going to have him.

He led her upstairs, neither of them speaking. It was as if a silent agreement had passed between them, neither of them wanting to speak in case it changed the atmosphere of heightened physical awareness.

He laid her on the old bed and she sank into the soft mattress, her bones melting as his dark eyes ran over her, lingering over her breasts, dipping to where her womanhood was secretly pulsing in anticipation of his invasion.

He pulled his T-shirt over his head and tossed it to the floor. Her stomach gave a funny little flip-flop when his hands went to his belt, the unclipping of the buckle the only sound in the room apart from her racing pulse which she was sure must be audible to him.

He stepped out of his trousers and his shoes thudded to the

floor as he came towards her, his eyes pinning her to the bed as surely as any bondage.

His fingers were gentle in their task to remove her clothes, so gentle she grew impatient and, brushing away his hand, she tore at them, wriggling out of them unashamedly.

He came down beside her on one knee, his hand stroking along her thigh, gradually going higher until his palm cupped her face once more. He lowered his mouth to hers in a lingering kiss, so leisurely she grew impatient. She nipped at his bottom lip and he suddenly stilled, his eyes growing darker as he looked down at her.

'I detect a tinge of impatience here.' His voice was a soft rumble against her breasts.

'I want you, Connor.' Her eyes held his without shame. 'Not tomorrow, not next week, but now.'

'Now it is.'

He reached for a condom and deftly positioned it before coming back over her, his thighs nudging hers apart.

'Are you sure about this?' he asked, searching her face for a sign of a change of mind. 'I don't want you to beat me over the head with this tomorrow when rationality returns.'

'I promise I won't.'

'I'm tempted—' he gave her body an intimate nudge '— but then, as I think about it—'

She grasped at him with clawing fingers.

'Connor, if you don't make love to me right this instant I'll call the press and tell them you're a lousy husband.'

He grinned down at her wickedly.

'I just love it when you beg.'

She would have said something but his body surged forward into her waiting warmth and all thoughts were immediately driven from her head. His groan of pleasure as her muscles enclosed him was like music to her ears, the weight of his body over hers a delight, the heat of his mouth a salve to her pride, knowing he wanted her just as much as she wanted him.

When his kiss deepened so too did his body in hers, driving her to a new level of feeling. Gone was the delicate brush of yesterday's tentative fingers. In their place were the ravenous hands of heightened desire, grabbing at their prize with greedy, insatiable fingers.

Jasmine almost screamed with the pleasure his lips and tongue called out of her. She was on fire, great leaping flames of desire licking at her flesh like a whip, scalding her until she could bear it no more. She wanted release but it was just out of reach. She had to climb and climb, but he kept her dangling until she was almost sobbing with her need.

'Please...' She nipped at his mouth and then his shoulder. 'Please, I want to...'

He slipped a hand down between their writhing bodies and found the swollen nub of her frantic desire, his touch gentle but determined. Jasmine sunk her teeth into his shoulder as the spasms hit her in great rolling waves that threatened to toss her to the floor of the ocean when they were over. She felt him tense as he prepared to let himself go, his body tight with sexual energy ready to burst forward.

He groaned his release beside her ear, sending delicious shudders of vicarious feeling through her. It made her feel so vital, so alive, so energised to think she had brought him to that.

He rolled to one side, his breathing still out of control.

'God.' He flung a hand over his eyes, his chest rising and falling as she watched him with hungry eyes. 'You're unbelievable.'

He rolled to his side in one fluid movement, propping himself up on one elbow to look at her.

'So are you.' She lowered her eyes, her shyness returning.

He hitched up her chin with one long finger.

'Hey, don't look away. I want to see that satisfied look in your eyes.'

She had no choice but to look at him.

'I'm sure you're very used to seeing very many satisfied women in your bed.'

'I prefer to concentrate on one at a time,' he said. 'And for now you're it.'

'For how long?' she couldn't stop herself from asking.

There was a funny little silence.

'For as long as it takes.'

She didn't know what to make of his answer. She supposed he was referring to the press interest. Perhaps he was planning to terminate their marriage once the hue and cry had died down.

She shut her eyes in case he could see her distress, her fingers plucking at the edge of the quilt in an absent manner.

'Don't worry, Jasmine.' His tone was teasing. 'I won't make you stay with me for ever if you don't want to.'

'I'm not the least bit worried,' she said tersely. 'I know this is a temporary arrangement.'

'It doesn't have to be temporary.'

Her eyes flew to his but his closed expression gave nothing away.

'What do you mean?' Her frown deepened.

'I mean we don't have to end our marriage unless we both want to.'

'But—' she bit her lip '—surely you won't want to tie yourself to me indefinitely?'

He shrugged noncommittally. 'It might be fun, you know, having kids and all.'

'You can't be serious!' She got off the bed in her agitation and snatched at the nearest article of clothing to cover herself.

'Why not?' His eyes sought hers. 'You think I won't be a good father?'

She opened and closed her mouth, uncertain how to respond.

'Well?'

A vision of him cradling a tiny dark-haired infant flitted

unbidden to her mind, his large hands gentle around the precious bundle.

'No.'

'No?'

'I mean yes, you'd make a wonderful father.'

'So what's the problem?'

'We don't love each other,' she said.

Another casual shrug. 'Most couples don't after a few years of marriage, so I can't see the problem.'

'Your cynicism is not reassuring.' She frowned at him.

He grinned. 'I know, but neither is the truth. More than two-thirds of all marriages end in divorce, most of them because one or the other has fallen out of love.'

'So where does that leave us?'

'It leaves us with a good chance of making a success of it because we haven't got the issue of blind love to cloud the issue.'

She bit her lip once more as she thought about his words. It was obvious he didn't love her, otherwise he'd have said so, surely?

'I don't think it's a good idea to bring a child into a relationship where hate is the dominant emotion,' she said, avoiding his eyes.

'You don't hate me, Jasmine.'

She lifted her chin, pride coming to her rescue. 'You seem very sure about that.'

'Sure enough.'

'Well, sorry to disappoint you but I'm very likely going to go to hell for the way I feel about you.'

He laughed. 'So am I.'

She couldn't stop her own smile at his wry tone.

'You find most things in life amusing, don't you?' she said.

'I find it pointless to torture myself with useless guilt and regret. We have one shot at life; my credo is to make it a good one.'

'So you flit from woman to woman in search of the ultimate physical experience?'

'You have a woeful view of my morality,' he quipped. 'I'm not a serial dater—I'm selective, that's all.'

'Am I supposed to be flattered?'

His mouth stretched into another quick, sexy grin. 'Of course.'

She looked away, not trusting herself not to give in to the temptation of returning to his bed and his arms for the pleasure promised in that smile.

'I think I'll have a bath,' she said.

'Want some company?'

She shook her head. 'The tub isn't big enough.'

'We can economise on space.' The wicked grin was back as was the twinkle in his dark eyes.

'Don't you ever think about anything else?' She scowled at him as she snatched at a bathrobe.

'Not much else when you're around,' he confessed unashamedly.

She felt a warm pool of pleasure fill her at his words but hastily reminded herself it was all about male physicality, nothing whatsoever to do with love.

The bathroom was cold but once she turned the hot tap on full it soon filled with steam and with a sigh she sank into the warmth of the water. As she soaped her body she couldn't stop herself from recalling how Connor's hands had explored every inch of her flesh in glorious mind-blowing detail. She lifted her leg free of the suds and immediately felt the pull of inner muscles and a quick spurt of remembered delight arrowed through her belly. She slid down beneath the water level.

She had to stop thinking about him all the time!

Was she so desperate for his attention that she'd put up with years of his womanising just so she could call herself his wife? That was surely the path to personal destruction.

How could she ignore his track record where women were concerned? If she did it would only come back to haunt her some time in the future, no doubt when he grew tired of her and went looking elsewhere. The thought of bringing a child into such a tenuous arrangement was beyond all rational thought. It was asking for trouble. The sort of trouble she had to deal with daily at the clinic. Broken people who turned to substance abuse to mask the pain of fractured relationships, bowed by bitterness and regret until they no longer functioned as normal people.

No. She was not going down that path.

She came up for air to find Connor looking down at her.

'You could have knocked!' She clutched at a face cloth to cover herself.

'I did but you were under the water.'

'You should have waited until I responded.'

'I thought I'd come in and wait for you to come up for air. The view is much nicer this side of the door.' His eyes ran over her thoroughly.

'You're being disgusting.'

'You're being unnecessarily coy.'

'I'm not being coy; I'm just not used to people waltzing into the bathroom when I'm having a bath.'

'I'm sure you'll get used to it in time.'

She gave him a black look. 'You have no respect for personal boundaries.'

'I have the greatest respect for your boundaries.' He trailed a long finger in the water right next to her thigh. The movement of the water where his finger disturbed the surface caressed her thigh in gentle laps, reminding her of the feel of his tongue...

'In fact,' he continued in a smoky tone, 'I was thinking about revisiting those boundaries.'

'Don't...' Her breath caught at the look in his dark eyes.

His finger moved up and traced the surface of the water in front of her breasts. He hadn't touched her once and yet she could feel herself melting, her intimate moisture gathering in anticipation.

It was a battle she could never win; she knew that and so did he, if the smouldering look he gave her was any judge.

She made room for him in the bath without a word. His eyes communicated his pleasure at her capitulation, lingering on her curves possessively until the blood ran thick and fast through her veins. He reached for her, sending a huge slosh of water over the sides, but she was beyond caring. His mouth was on hers, his hands were on her body, his thighs were between hers—this was heaven.

Her head thumped on the back of the bath as he sent her backwards with his first forceful thrust but she made no demur. She welcomed him with abandon, her limbs stretching apart to give him more room. He took her with him on a tidal wave of passion, his hands and mouth joining in the task of delivering her at ecstasy's door with harsh cries of release echoing his own.

The bathroom floor looked as if someone had left a tap on. Connor lay back in the almost empty tub and eyed it ruefully.

'You're one messy woman. Look at that.'

She gave him a playful poke in the ribs with her big toe.

'How like a man to blame someone else for the mess they made themselves.'

He caught her foot and gave her toe a quick hard suck, sending shudders of sensation along her spine.

'Hey!' She wriggled ineffectually. 'Let me go. That tickles!'

He sucked harder.

'Connor, I'm warning you,' she gasped. 'I can't think straight when you do that.'

'I don't want you to think straight,' he growled, dropping her foot to reach for her arms to haul her upwards towards him. 'I want you to think crookedly, sinfully, shamelessly— like me.'

She felt the unmistakable pulse of his growing erection between her legs as she slid on to his chest, but it was the only thought she had for quite some time…

Jasmine woke in the early hours of the morning. It was still dark but the moon made several brief appearances before the curtains of cloud created another interval for its performance.

She lay and watched Connor relaxed in sleep. His breathing was deep and even, his long frame taking up far too much room in the bed, but she wasn't going to wake him by pointing out that fact. Without his penetrating gaze to disturb her she could drink her fill of his features.

She sighed and allowed herself the luxury of reaching out a hand to his chest where his heart lay beating, her fingers nestling against the light sprinkle of masculine hair.

He muttered something in his sleep and turned over, taking her hand with him. She was right up against his back, her legs fitting in the crook of his, her cold body soaking up his tempting warmth…

Connor woke to the soft murmur of her voice near his ear. At first it was just a few indistinguishable sounds, nothing he could make any sense of. But then it changed. Her body tightened, her limbs rigid with fear as the nightmare took hold, her desperate cries filling all four corners of the room.

'Jasmine.' He shook her gently. 'Honey, wake up.'

'No!' She tossed her head as she thrust against his restraining hands. 'No!'

'Baby,' he soothed. 'Hey, it's just a dream; you're having a bad dream.'

She opened her eyes and stared at him blankly for a few seconds.

'Hey, sweetheart, you were having a nightmare.'

She pushed against his hands and got out of the bed, her body stiff as she faced him.

'You should have woken me.'

He gave her a bewildered look. 'I was doing my best.'

She turned away, her arms tight across her chest at the chill of the room.

'What did I say?' she asked, still with her back to him.

'Nothing I could make any sense of,' he answered.

She turned around to glare at him through the pallid light of the reappearing moon.

'Are you telling me the truth?'

'Of course I'm telling the truth. Why would I lie?'

'Because lying is second nature to you, that's why.'

He frowned. 'Jasmine, I know sharing a bed with someone is new to you but people say and do things in their sleep all the time. It's no great drama, believe me.'

'It is to me.'

'What are you trying to hide?'

'Nothing.'

'Then you've got nothing to worry about. Now come back to bed before you turn to ice out there.'

'I don't want to come back to bed.'

'I promise I won't touch you.' His tone was growing impatient as he switched on the lamp. 'Just get back in the damn bed before I lose my temper.'

'Lose your temper, I don't care.'

He thrust the quilt aside with an angry scowl.

'All right then.' His feet hit the floor with an ominous thud. 'You've asked for it.'

Jasmine stood her ground, determined not to be intimidated by him. He came to stand in front of her, glaring down at her in the soft lighting of the bedside lamp.

'I'm in no mood for this push and pull game you're so intent on playing,' he growled.

'I'm in no mood for your games either,' she shot back.

'Fine.' He held his hands up in the air in a gesture of surrender. 'I promise not to touch you, OK? I just want you to get back in the bed and go back to sleep. That's it, all right?'

She felt a bubble of emotion spring in her chest and, before she could stop them, two tears squeezed past the tight clamp of her eyes.

'Oh, for God's sweet sake.' He reached for her and hauled her into the shelter of his warm chest.

She sobbed against his thudding heart, all her normal control disappearing as if he'd turned a switch.

'Hey, this is new,' he mused as he stroked the silk of her hair. 'I've never seen you cry before.'

'It's not a show!' she howled.

'I know that,' he soothed, his palm gentle against the back of her head. 'I'm just surprised you trust me enough to let your guard down.'

'I don't trust you,' she sobbed.

'I know you don't think you do but you do underneath, where it counts.'

'I don't! I don't trust anyone!'

'Yes, you do.' His voice was like a caress as he held her against him. 'You just don't like admitting it.'

'I want to be alone.'

'No, you don't.'

'You don't know what I want.'

'Yes, I do.'

'I hate you.'

'No, you don't.'

'I do so.'

'You don't.'

'I don't want to talk to you.'

'Then don't talk.'

She looked up at him through tear-washed eyes.

'Why are you so annoying?'

He smiled. 'Because it's my job.'

'You're fired.'

He laughed and gathered her back into his chest.

'Jasmine, I'm sure I'm getting laughter lines just because of you.'

She didn't know what to say in response. He had the most

disarming manner at times, dissolving anger in a matter of seconds with a phrase that sent a smile to her lips and another arrow of love to her heart.

'I wish I'd never met you,' she said, not meaning it at all.

'I know.' He laced his fingers through the silk of her hair. 'I know exactly what you mean.' He tilted her chin and planted a soft kiss on the bow of her mouth.

She sighed into his mouth, her limbs already loosening at the probe of his determined tongue. What was the point in fighting it? She was his for as long as he wanted her and surely that was all that mattered?

CHAPTER TEN

WHEN she woke the next time she was alone in the bed. The birds outside the window were chirping with the vigour of early morning energy, a type of energy she couldn't help envying.

Her body felt languorous, sleepy and contented from the early morning activity Connor had insisted would be a sure cure for her insomnia. It had certainly worked for him for within minutes of their passionate exchange he'd been asleep, his arms still around her, his legs still entwined with hers.

Her own sleep had been slightly less forthcoming. She'd lain looking at the shadows of dawn dancing across the ceiling until they were shadows no more but streaks of golden light.

Connor had sighed and turned her over with him in a single movement. She'd closed her eyes and breathed in the scent of him, wondering how many mornings she had allotted to her before he would be on to new, more exciting, pastures.

They spent the next few days in much the same way. Jasmine went for long walks along the seashore while he worked on the house. Occasionally he'd join her at the tail end of her walk, his arm slung casually around her shoulders, his smile frequent as he recounted some anecdote that brought a reluctant smile to her own mouth.

She liked watching him work. Having grown up with a father who thought handyman tasks beneath his theological intellect, it was quite a novelty for Jasmine to see Connor up and down a ladder while he repaired a crack in the plaster of a high wall or ceiling. Sometimes she handed him a tool from the toolbox at the foot of the ladder, her fingers touching his as she held it up to him. His dark eyes would send her a silent message as he took the instrument and she would look away, frightened he'd be able to see the desperate longing reflected in her gaze.

The nights they shared with a passion she hadn't known she'd been capable of. Time and time again he delivered her to the threshold of fulfilment with him in hot pursuit, their groans of delight a single sound. It made her shiver every time she recalled the way he collapsed against her, his great body wrecked by passion spent.

Tuesday came before she wanted it to. With it came the realisation that their privacy would end abruptly as they each took up their responsibilities once more.

The drive back to town was silent by tacit agreement. Jasmine sat and thought about her work at the clinic and wondered how she'd juggle her new role as Connor's wife while supporting the needy the way she'd done previously. The hours she worked were unforgiving at times, leaving her worn out both physically and emotionally, and within the context of their sudden marriage she knew she might have to make some adjustments.

She sneaked a glance his way once or twice but if he was worried about his own adjustments he showed no sign of it. He drove with quiet competence all the way up the freeway and then on to the highway interchange.

Finally they arrived at his house in Woollahra and once the car had stopped she got out and stretched her legs before he could get to her door.

He took their bags from the rear of the car as she went to open the front door with the key he'd given her previously.

Before she could use the key the housekeeper, Maria, opened the door and greeted her in rapid fire broken English. Jasmine caught one or two words that sounded a little like Italian but she wasn't sure.

Connor came up behind her and smiled at the older woman.

He proceeded to speak in the other woman's language, which made Jasmine turn her head to stare at him.

He caught her surprised expression and flashed a quick grin.

'I learnt to speak it when I lived in Sicily for six months.'

He turned back to the housekeeper and made brief introductions. Jasmine held out her hand and it was taken humbly by the older woman, who said something in her strange, unintelligible dialect.

Jasmine turned to Connor for an interpretation, her brow clouded with uncertainty.

'Maria speaks a little English but it's slow and it embarrasses her. I'll teach you a few phrases to get you through but for the time being just smile and nod your head as if you understand.'

She turned back to the housekeeper and smiled shyly. Connor said something in Italian and Maria's face lit up as she scuttled away to do whatever it was he suggested.

'What did you say to her?' Jasmine looked up at him.

'I told her to have the rest of the day off.'

'Why?'

His eyes twinkled with mischief.

'Because I want you to myself, that's why.'

Her stomach somersaulted as he reached for her, his mouth coming down on hers before she could say a word. He pressed her back against the nearest wall, his hands feeling her breasts through her thin sweater where her heart was leaping towards the warmth of his spread palm.

He was like a drug in her system. She could never have enough of him and with every kiss her need increased until she was breathless with wanting. She tore at his shirt with needy fingers, wanting the silk of his flesh beneath her fingertips, wanting to shape him intimately from head to foot as he had to her.

He tore his mouth off hers and, scooping her effortlessly into his arms, carried her up the stairs, shouldering open his bedroom door. Jasmine's breath was caught somewhere in the back of her throat at the look of masculine intent in his dark eyes.

He laid her on the bed and finished the task she'd begun of removing his shirt. His trousers were next and then his under shorts. He came towards her, his eyes dark with desire while hers widened in anticipation. His hands went to the waistband of her jeans and she lay back, stretching her arms above her head as he bent his head to her belly button, his tongue dipping into its tiny cave. A whirlpool of shivery sensations spiralled through her as his warm mouth moved lower to seek her feminine folds, separating them delicately, intruding into the dark secrecy of her core with bold strokes, leaving her writhing in exultant ecstasy.

He moved over her once more, lifting her sweater out of the path of his mouth and hands. She arched her back as his tongue circled her tight nipples in turn, the knife-hot feel of him against her a torture in itself.

She touched him, shaping him with fingers that trembled in their task. He sucked in his breath as she intensified the movement, lingering over his most sensitive spot until he grabbed at her hand and, holding it above her head, entered her with a harsh grunt of pleasure as her tender form caught and held him tight.

She was on another journey to paradise as his body stroked hers with deep, pulsing strokes, drawing from her a response she could never withhold even if she'd wanted to for pride's sake. Her cries of release were beyond suppressing as they leapt from her throat in high, gasping sounds that, when over, left her breathless and spent in his embrace.

Connor timed his own release, leaving it until she was supine in his arms before letting himself fall towards oblivion in deep throbbing waves that shook him to the core of his being.

He lay listening to the soft sound of Jasmine's breathing and wondered why it had taken him till now to finally realise

he loved her. He'd kidded himself he desired her just as he'd
desired many women in the past, but who was he fooling
now? Her heart was beating against his, her body was curled
into him and her feminine scent was like a drug he had to
breathe in just to survive.

She shifted in his arms, her chin burrowing into his chest
as she searched for warmth.

He trickled his fingers through the silky curtain of hair and
speculated on what she'd say if he woke her to tell her. But
then he remembered there were other things she needed to
know and, besides, he didn't want to be the one to burst her
bubble. But he was going to make damn sure he was there to
help her pick up the pieces.

When Jasmine arrived at the clinic the next morning she was
a little unprepared for the intrusive interest her sudden marriage had stirred amongst the other staff and even some of the
clients. She spent most of the morning fielding questions with
as much tact as she could manage but towards the end of the
afternoon she was getting to the point of screaming. It wasn't
hard to pretend she was in love, for she was; it was more
because every time she thought about Connor she was assailed
by a sinking feeling of hopelessness as she recalled his mo-
tivations for marrying her. He'd married her to secure his late
mother's estate—nothing more, nothing less. It was about
money, not his feelings.

She had only been home a few minutes when the telephone
rang.

'Jasmine! You sly old thing!' her sister Sam exclaimed. 'I
couldn't believe it when Mum told me you and Connor were
married!'

'Yes, well, it's been rather a shock to most people.'

'I thought you didn't like him?' Sam said.

'I don't—didn't,' she said. 'But things are different now.'

'Love is like that,' Sam rattled on happily. 'I didn't like

Finn the first time I saw him either but one kiss and that was it—whammo! Love, lust and—'

'How was the honeymoon?' Jasmine cut across her sister's intimate revelation.

'Great.' Sam's tone was instantly dreamy. 'Everything I could have wished for, in fact.'

'Lucky you.'

'I guess Connor didn't have much time to organise a honeymoon?'

'No.'

'He's a great guy, Jasmine. I'm sure you'll be very happy.'

'Yes.'

'You're not still upset with Mum and Dad, are you?'

'Why should I be upset?'

'I heard they were pretty strong on the idea of marriage, given you'd been found in his bed.'

'There was a certain amount of pressure, yes.'

Sam giggled.

'I think it's terribly romantic, don't you? The outraged parents insisting on the poor man making an honest woman out of you, just like in one of those Victorian dramas.'

'Yes, it was very romantic.'

'You shouldn't take too much notice of what Mum and Dad think about him,' Sam advised. 'He's not the man he's been made out to be, if you know what I mean.'

'I know exactly what you mean.'

'I thought you would. I mean, he hasn't had it all that easy with his mother dying so young and no father and so on. He was left with nothing, not a penny. He had to depend on the charity of Julian and Harriet until he could make his own fortune, which he did rather spectacularly. He's incredibly wealthy now.'

Jasmine frowned as she took in her sister's words.

'But I thought his mother left an estate?'

'No, Finn told me about it just recently. He'd overheard his parents discussing it. Anyway, even if there was money,

Harriet would've spent it by now. Did you see the outfit she wore to the wedding? Finn told me how much it cost. Phew! I couldn't believe it when I heard.'

Jasmine needed time to think.

'Sam, I have to go. I've left something on the stove.'

'Call me soon,' Sam said cheerily. 'I want to show you the wedding photographs. There's a great one of you looking daggers at Connor at the reception. It will be great to show your children one day.'

Jasmine replaced the receiver once Sam had trilled her last goodbye and sat heavily on the nearest sofa, her hands shaking as she clasped them in her lap.

He'd lied to her. He'd expressly told her he needed to be married to access his mother's money. He'd tricked her into a loveless, pointless marriage. How had she fallen so neatly in with his plans? She felt like kicking herself for her own blind stupidity. He'd seized the opportunity when her parents had applied a bit of pressure, concocting his own tale of woe to draw her in. She'd fallen for it so gullibly. It made her sick to think of how easy it had been for him to get her to do what he had wanted. How he must be laughing at her behind her back. He couldn't have chosen a better victim. Who better than a high profile young woman such as herself, with a tainted reputation to match—a Bishop's wayward daughter, who had already caused one man's career to tumble. She'd been an easy target for his ruthless machinations, and to add to his victory she'd foolishly fallen in love with him. She'd even allowed him to make love to her, filling her head with stupid, empty dreams of happy-ever-afters that could never be.

Connor turned his key in the lock whilst balancing his briefcase under his other arm. His temples were tight with a tension headache which had grown steadily worse as the day had progressed.

He'd met his stepfather that morning to discuss accessing

his mother's estate, handing Julian his marriage certificate with an element of pride. His stepfather, however, had dismissed him with a wave of one hand.

'You surely don't think there's any of your mother's money left after all this time, do you?' Julian looked at him from beneath his grey bushy brows.

Connor felt himself stiffen.

'She left it to me,' he said. 'I'm here to collect it.'

Julian shuffled some papers on his desk, something in his manner suggesting he wasn't entirely comfortable with the discussion.

'I'm sure I don't need to remind you of the costs in raising a child,' he said. 'And since you were expelled from several schools the fees we had to pay for the Academy had to be met somehow.'

Connor's frown deepened.

'You mean there's nothing left?'

'Your mother wanted you to have a good education,' Julian said. 'I felt I owed it to her to ensure you got one even though you were hell-bent on sabotaging it at every opportunity.'

Connor had left his stepfather's rooms in an anger induced daze. He didn't trust Julian's explanation but knew that unless he was prepared to take him on in a court case he had no guarantee of winning he had no choice but to accept it as a lesson well learnt.

The only trouble was that his primary reason for marrying Jasmine no longer existed. And if she were to ever find out…

He closed the door behind him and, tossing his keys to the hall table, ran a hand through his hair, squinting against the pain across his forehead.

'Good day at the office?' Jasmine's tone was cool as she stepped out from the shadow of the sitting room doorway.

'Oh, hello, Jasmine.' He winced as his head gave another sickening pound. 'You would not believe the day I've had.' He shrugged himself out of his coat and flung it towards the hall stand with another flinch of pain.

'I'm sure I wouldn't.'

His eyes went to hers. 'Is everything all right?'

'What could possibly be wrong?' She held his narrowed-eyed look.

He ran a hand across his eyes and sighed.

'I have the most appalling headache.'

'Poor you.'

He hunted her face for the sincerity he'd sensed had been lacking in her tone.

'Has someone upset you?' he asked after a tiny pause.

'Who would do such a thing?' she asked.

'I don't know; your parents, perhaps?'

'I haven't spoken to my parents since the wedding.'

'Who have you been talking to?'

'No one you'd be interested in.'

'I don't know about that.' He loosened his tie. 'Why don't you tell me and I'll be the judge?'

'I was talking to my sister.'

'Sam?'

She gave a single nod.

'Finn called me too. Seems they had a great time,' he said, leading the way into the kitchen.

She stood silently watching him as he took a glass from the cupboard and filled it with water. He pressed two pain-killers from a foil strip and tossed back his head to swallow them.

'God, I feel like a construction team has started up inside my head,' he said, rubbing a hand across his forehead.

'My heart bleeds.'

He frowned, then leant his hips back against the bench and looked at her closely.

'At the risk of repeating myself, are you all right?'

She lifted her chin a fraction. 'You seem very determined that something must be wrong. Why, Connor? Is your con-science pricking you?'

His eyes fell away from hers as he put the glass down.

'I'm not sure what you're talking about but no doubt you're going to enlighten me.'

She drew in an angry breath. 'Why did you lie to me?'

'About what?' His eyes came back to hers, but this time she noted they were clouded with wariness.

'Lots of things, but the one that immediately springs to mind is the true nature of your financial affairs.'

There was a pulsing silence.

'You lied to me about your mother's estate, didn't you?' She glared at him furiously.

He didn't answer but she could see the flare of guilt in his dark eyes.

'You told me you needed to get married to access your late mother's estate.'

'I know what I said.'

'There is no estate, is there, Connor?'

He drew in a breath. 'Not any more.'

'There never was!' She threw the words at him. 'You lied to me to make me do what you wanted. I should have seen it from the start but I was fool enough to fall...to fall for it,' she tacked on quickly.

'Jasmine, you're jumping to the sort of conclusions you're very likely to regret when I explain—'

'I don't want your explanations or your bare-faced lies! I don't want anything from you but the truth, but you can't do that, can you? You wouldn't know how to tell the truth if it were tattooed on your tongue!'

'Oh, for God's sake!' Connor slammed his fist against the bench in frustration. 'Will you let me tell you my side of this?'

'Do you think I even care what story you're busily rehearsing in your head?'

'I'm not rehearsing anything.' He raked a hand through his hair. 'I intended telling you eventually, but I only found out about it—'

'Eventually?' She threw him a fulminating look. 'You

should have told me before I was stupid enough to sign my name on that marriage certificate!'

He needed time to think.

Her anger was justified, he knew, but he wanted to be in a better frame of mind than he currently was before he explained.

He garnered his pride with an effort and glared back at her. 'What is this? I come home with a fierce headache to this!'

'You shouldn't have come home at all,' she said bitterly. 'You should have gone to your latest lover's waiting arms instead.'

His eyes flashed with some indefinable emotion.

'Well, then.' His voice was a harsh scratch of sound in his throat. 'Maybe that's exactly what I will do.'

CHAPTER ELEVEN

JASMINE stared after his stiff back when Connor strode from the room, flinching as the woodwork protested as he slammed the door behind him. If a confession was what she was after she was sure she'd just received it; she'd never seen someone so guilty in all her life.

He didn't come home that night or the night after. Jasmine carried on as if nothing was the matter, mostly for appearance's sake, under the watchful, silent gaze of Maria the housekeeper.

She filled her days at the clinic, working a double shift to keep from facing the aching emptiness of Connor's house. She tortured herself with images of him with someone else— a tall, leggy blonde with a figure to die for, or a raven-haired temptress with smouldering eyes.

On the evening of the third day she'd had enough. She called the clinic and told them she needed some time off and, quickly packing a bag, made her way to the garage where the second of Connor's cars was parked.

The drive to the south coast was lengthened by the snarl of traffic at the start of the freeway due to an accident. She drummed her fingers on the steering wheel impatiently as she waited for the tow truck to clear the debris.

The old house was cold and dark, its shadowy verandas like heavy brows over sightless eyes.

She unlocked the door and after carrying her few things in shut it behind her, breathing in the empty silence.

She turned on one small light, somehow content with the creeping darkness. She struck a match to the fire Connor had left laid ready in the fireplace and waited for its warmth to seep into the stiff coldness of her bones.

It was hard to sit in front of the flames without thinking of him. She could almost feel his touch, the slide of his warm fingers down her arm, the rasp of his unshaven jaw on her breasts as she lay in his embrace.

She sighed as she poked at the fire once or twice. She'd have to learn to live without him, that was all.

She woke to the dawn chorus and her own low spirits. The sun was a pale imitation of its usual self, which did nothing to lift her low mood. The old house seemed to creak around her with every step she took within it, as if it were asking her, Where is he? Where is he?

In the end, she gave up and went for a long walk along the beach, striding with a vigour she couldn't feel through the heavy sand. The thunderous waves pounded at the shore in great lashing strokes, trying to soak her feet as she went past. The air was fresh with sea spray and the hoarse cries of the gulls echoed the silent cries of her heart as she faced the prospect of a future alone.

When she got back to the house she picked at some scraps of food she'd brought with her with little enthusiasm. Everything she touched reminded her of Connor. She saw his smile reflected in the glass of the windows, tasted his kiss on the afternoon breeze against her lips, felt his presence in the big bed when she lay down and tried to force herself to sleep. He was everywhere; she couldn't escape, for she'd brought him with her in her heart.

Some time during the night something woke her. At first she thought it must have been a possum on the roof but when she sat up to listen there was no sound except the soft brush of the branches of the old elm tree outside the bedroom window.

She watched the play of moonlit shadows on the ceiling for a while before finally giving up on the whole notion of further sleep. She threw back the bedcovers and, wrapping herself in the bathrobe Connor had left behind, made her way in moonlit darkness to the library to find something to read to take her mind off her worries.

The library floor creaked in protest as she stepped into the room. The rows of books seemed to have developed accusing eyes as they looked down at who had disturbed their solitude.

Jasmine gave herself a mental shake and switched on the desk lamp, but the sensation of being watched remained.

She reached for the book nearest her, which happened to be a family Bible, its spine encrusted with gold. Pulling out a chair and tucking her feet underneath her, she sat with the Bible in her lap and began turning the yellowed pages with careful fingers.

A single photograph fluttered to the floor as she turned from Genesis to Exodus. She reached down and, picking it up, turned it over and froze.

It was a photograph of her.

The heavy Bible slipped from her knees as she unfolded her legs, her startled eyes still on the photograph in her shaking hands.

She knew the photograph well. It was exactly the same as the one in the photograph album her mother had made her for her tenth birthday. She was a few months old, lying on a rug in a garden she didn't recognise, rosy cheeks and her wide, mostly toothless, smile.

How had it come to be between the leaves of this particular Bible? A host of questions flew around her brain, but none of the answers she needed.

She picked up the Bible and began leafing through the rest of the fragile pages, past Leviticus, Numbers, Deuteronomy and then on to Joshua and Judges. Another photograph was pressed between the pages of Ruth. This time she was a little older, a year or so, and the garden she did recognise as that of her childhood home.

There was another photograph of her in 1 and 2 Chronicles, one in Proverbs, a school photograph in Hosea and her confirmation photograph in the New Testament section between Acts and Romans.

She put the Bible back down and leafed through the collection of photographs in her trembling hands, her mind whirling with a magnitude of unanswerable questions.

After what seemed hours, she suddenly sprang to her feet, tossing the photographs to one side. She stared at the rows of books in front of her for a moment, before she began pulling them at random from the shelves, her fingers searching through the pages of every single volume.

She found a lock of curly chestnut hair in Charles Dickens' *Great Expectations*. She stared at it for endless minutes, her brain darting off in all directions but unable to make sense of it.

She put the lock of hair to one side and ran her eyes along the top shelves where the last books remained.

Only one book along the row had no gold-embossed title on its spine.

She reached for it with nerveless fingers, somehow not all that surprised to find it was a diary.

She sat on the dusty sofa and, taking a painful breath, turned the first page.

It was addressed to God.

I saw her today.

She came to the house on her way to the beach. I wanted to call out to her but, as you know, I gave up that right a long time ago.

At least I have the photos. She looks so like me, which I suppose is a rough sort of justice. How that must annoy your avid disciple!

You'd better look after her while I'm gone. She's the only thing I'm proud of in my life. The one thing I did properly. I would have loved to have kept her but I was told you wouldn't approve.

As for me, I'm not so sure…

Jasmine sat in the quiet stillness of the old house, cradling the diary in her hands, her eyes moving over the various entries to find out the identity of the owner but to no avail—the diary was as anonymous as the 'disciple' referred to within it.

She knew she could put it off no longer; the creeping shadows of doubt could not be contained any more. She had to know the truth, even though she knew it was going to be painful.

She knew she had to visit her parents and ask them who would be watching her from afar, entering details about her in a nameless diary, for who but they was likely to know?

With that resolution in mind she tucked the photographs and diary beneath her pillow and shut her eyes, willing herself to sleep.

Her mother answered the door first thing the next morning with her hair still in the soft rollers she customarily wore to bed.

'Jasmine!' She put her hand to the plastic assortment on her head in what Jasmine knew to be a nervous gesture.

'Hello, Mum.'

'Darling, you don't have to knock,' her mother chided as she ushered her inside. 'Just because you're married now doesn't mean you're not our daughter any more.'

Jasmine couldn't have asked for a better opening.

'But I'm not your daughter, am I?'

Frances Byrne visibly blanched.

'I…I don't know what you mean, darling.' She recovered quickly. 'Is…is everything all right between you and Connor?'

'I'm not here to discuss my…Connor,' Jasmine said firmly. 'I've come to discuss these.' She handed her mother the small clutch of photographs but kept the leather-bound diary in her bag.

Frances took the photographs with an unsteady hand.

Jasmine watched as she turned each one over, her expression clouding as each image was revealed.

There was a hollow silence.

After a few moments her mother handed her back the photographs, carefully avoiding her eyes.

'I can't imagine where you found those,' she said, dusting off her hands.

'Can't you?'

Frances disturbed the neat perfection of her coral lipstick with her teeth.

'Darling, your father will be very sorry he missed you and, as you see, I'm getting ready to go to church and—'

'I want to know the truth,' Jasmine said. 'The gospel truth.'

'Darling—' her mother's hands fluttered near her throat '—I'm not sure I can handle you in this mood.'

'I'm not leaving here until I have the truth,' Jasmine said implacably. 'And if you won't speak to me here then I'll have to go to the synod gathering and have it out with Father there.'

'Oh, dear Lord, don't do that!' Desperation crept into her mother's voice.

'Why ever not?' Jasmine asked. 'He's my father, isn't he? Surely I should be able to call him out of a meeting to speak with me?'

The silence this time was agonising.

'Darling—' her mother's face was pale with anguish as she wrung her hands '—your father and I—'

'Leave this to me, Frances.' Elias Byrne's voice sounded from behind Jasmine.

She spun around to find her father standing in the open doorway.

'I hope you've got a very good explanation for coming here and upsetting your mother like this.' He closed the door behind him with an ominous click.

Jasmine refused to be intimidated.

'I want to know the truth. Surely you owe me that?'

'We've taught you the truth since you were an infant but you've wilfully and rebelliously refused to acknowledge it.'

'Not that sort of truth!' Tears smarted in her eyes. 'Why must you always preach at me?'

'You've got a defiant streak, Jasmine. We've done all we can to school you out of it but it seems you're determined to ignore our admonitions.'

'I didn't come here for a sermon.' Jasmine's tone was cold. 'I want you to tell me why those photographs of me were in a family Bible in the old house next to the shack at Pelican Head.'

Her parents exchanged glances.

Elias's face drained of colour and her mother's hand fluttered back to her string of pearls.

'I'm not leaving until I know the truth,' Jasmine added determinedly.

After a stretching silence her father appeared to come to some sort of decision. He straightened his spine and met her defiant grey-blue gaze with the cool ice blue of his own.

'All right, then.' He ignored the choked sound from Frances beside him. 'I'll tell you the truth but you must promise me it is to go no further than the four walls of this room.'

She hated having to make such a promise but she needed to know so desperately. She nodded her head, her stomach churning as she waited for him to continue.

Elias disturbed the neat comb-over he'd perfected that morning with a nervous flick of his hand.

'It's true that you're not our biological daughter,' he said. 'Your mother and I adopted you when you were six weeks old.'

Jasmine stared at them both.

'We would have told you but when Samantha came along a few months later you both looked so alike and we thought it best for all concerned to retain the secrecy. Of course, now you and the girls are all grown up the differences between you are more marked than we would have liked, but—'

'So sorry not to have fitted in as you wanted,' Jasmine put in bitterly.

Her father's brows drew together in a frown.

'Your propensity to speak before you think is one of those differences. It got your mother into trouble too, which is why we offered to take you in.'

'Who is my mother?'

'Your mother is dead.'

Jasmine's stomach hollowed.

'I still want to know who she was.'

Elias and Frances exchanged glances once more.

'Your mother was a rebellious drug addict who found herself pregnant. She gave you up and soon after disappeared. We've since heard that she had passed away some time ago.'

Jasmine felt as if the world was spinning out of control within the confines of her head.

'What about my father?' she managed to ask through the cold stiffness of her lips. 'Who was he?'

'We were never told his name. Your mother wouldn't say.'

She absorbed this information for a moment or two in silence.

'As for the photographs, I have no idea how they came to be where you said they were. Perhaps it's one of those coincidences that just happens from time to time,' Elias offered.

'*A coincidence?*' Jasmine frowned heavily.

'Of course—' he was obviously pleased with his explanation '—perhaps someone bought the Bible at a second-hand store or church fair and didn't check inside.'

'You surely can't expect me to believe in that sort of coincidence?'

'You have always shown a deplorable lack of faith in the miraculous,' Elias pointed out. 'But I have no idea how the photographs were obtained, do you, Frances?'

Frances shook her head, her eyes bright with tears.

Jasmine took out the diary and handed it to them both.

'What's this?' Elias frowned.

'It's a diary,' she said.

'Whose diary?' He turned a few pages with fumbling fingers.

'I was hoping you could tell me,' she said.

She watched as his throat moved up and down in an agitated swallow and assumed he'd come to the 'avid disciple' entry.

Elias handed the diary back, meticulously avoiding her eye as he did so.

'I realise this has come as somewhat of a shock to you but you must believe us when we tell you we kept the details of your birth quiet with the very best of intentions. You had no future with your mother; she was beyond redemption. We took you in as our own. Your mother—Frances, I mean—' he gave his wife a brief glance '—had not long had a miscarriage and was feeling low. You were a wonderful solution to her unhappiness and brought us much joy in those early years.'

But not in latter years. Jasmine filled in the rest in her head.

'Darling, no one else needs to know about this.' Frances was struggling to hold back her emotion. 'It would upset your sisters terribly if they were to find out at this late stage.'

'What about me?' Jasmine's own tears sprang to her eyes. 'Am I not allowed to be upset?'

'It's understandable under the circumstances, but—' Elias began.

'You don't mind upsetting me because I'm not really your daughter, but we mustn't upset the girls because they are? How unfair is that? Don't you understand how this is for me?'

'Of course we do but surely you must understand how difficult this is,' Frances said. 'Your father and I—'

'Don't call yourselves that!' Jasmine almost screamed the words at them. 'You're not my parents.'

'Darling, please—'

'Jasmine, control yourself. You're a married woman now, not a teenage girl. Go home to your husband and be grateful for the life you've had; it was a whole lot more promising than your birth mother had to offer.'

Jasmine wrenched the front door open and slammed it behind her, almost stumbling down the front steps with blinding, bitter tears. She drove away with a squeal of tyres she knew would annoy her father—no Elias Byrne, her adopted father, she corrected herself with another choking sob.

She drove around in circles, not sure whether she should go back to the old house or drive straight to Connor's place. So many questions were leaping in her head, each one vying for her attention, but she could barely think straight let alone attempt to frame any answers.

As she did another round of the block she recalled the cryptic comment Connor had made when he'd shown her the library at the old house for the first time. She'd told him the old books were very likely priceless and he'd said, *'I'm sure one or two will prove to be so.'*

She gnawed at her lip, trying to decipher the meaning of his words. Had he known something? Had he stumbled across the photographs and diary himself or had he known the previous occupant of the house? She had to know, even if it meant facing him again, which she wasn't sure she wanted to do right now.

Her curiosity got the better of her. She turned the car at the next roundabout and tracked back across the flow of traffic to make her way to Woollahra, determined to have it out with him.

When she arrived, she was relieved to find Connor's car in the garage and made her way to the front door, mentally rehearsing what she wanted to say. She went to unlock the door but before she could put the key in the lock it opened and he stood before her.

'Jasmine, I need to talk to you.'

She brushed past him to enter the house, not sure she wanted to pick up the threads of their last conversation just yet; she had more pressing things on her mind.

'I want to apologise.'

Her head came around at that. He sounded genuine but she wasn't quite sure what he was apologising for. Was it for not telling her the truth about his mother's estate or for his abrupt manner when he'd stormed from the house the other evening?

'I see.'

'No, you don't see.'

She followed him into the sitting room, where he proceeded to pour two generous shots of brandy. She took hers but didn't lift it to her mouth, simply cradling it in her hands as she faced him.

He ran a hand through his already disordered hair.

'I was out of line the other night,' he began. 'I had the mother of all headaches and when you threw the issue of my mother's estate in my face, I lost it.'

'You lied to me.'

'I didn't lie to you.'

'You expect me to believe you?'

'Yes.' He thrust his own glass aside untouched. 'I'd like to explain about my mother's estate.'

'Please don't put yourself to any bother.' Her tone was laced with scorn.

'Jasmine, I know you think the worst of me right now but I can explain.'

'Go right ahead.' She gave him the floor with a theatrical sweep of her hand. 'God knows I could do with another good story after what I've already heard today.'

'What have you heard?'

She turned away. 'Nothing that's relevant to this conversation.'

'Jasmine, there's something you should know—'

'Why did you lie to me about your mother's estate?'

'Until a few days ago I didn't even know my mother's estate no longer existed.'

She wasn't sure she wanted to believe him but something

in his tone suggested he found the task of speaking about it difficult, so she stayed silent.

'But I want you to know that even if I had found out in time I would still have wanted to marry you.'

'Why?' she asked. 'Why did you want to marry me?'

His eyes shifted away from hers. 'I wanted to settle down.'

'With me?'

'Why not you?'

'I'm hardly perfect wife material.'

'I don't know about that and, besides, I'm not the perfect catch either, so what's the problem?'

'The problem is I'm not who you think I am.'

'I know you're not the wayward rebel people have made you out to be.'

'I don't mean that.' She chanced a quick glance at his face. 'I mean I'm not really a bishop's daughter.'

His dark eyes meshed with hers.

'Whose daughter are you?'

She lowered her gaze. 'I don't know.'

'I see.'

'No, you don't see,' she said, not caring that they'd each recycled each other's words several times in the space of a few minutes. 'I'm not my parents' daughter.'

'Do you have any idea whose daughter you might be?'

She couldn't meet his eyes.

'I don't know,' she answered raggedly. 'I don't know.'

She heard him move across the room and the chink of a bottle against a glass as he topped up his brandy.

'I take it Elias and Frances didn't enlighten you?'

She felt almost grateful he hadn't referred to them as her parents.

'No,' she said hollowly. 'They didn't enlighten me.'

'And Sam, Caitlin, Bianca—do they know about this?'

She shook her head, not trusting herself to speak.

'I see,' he said again.

She seriously questioned that; how could he possibly know what she was going through?

'I don't know what to do,' she found herself confessing. 'I've always suspected something wasn't quite right in my family but I could never put my finger on exactly what.'

'They should've told you.'

She bit her lip as she thought about her parents' dilemma.

'They did what they thought was best, I see that now.'

'You're very gracious.'

'You wouldn't say that if you heard what I said to them a few hours ago.'

'It's been such a shock,' he said. 'It's understandable.'

She sat down on the nearest sofa with a heavy sigh. 'I feel like an alien.'

'You don't have green skin, if that's any consolation.'

She couldn't stop her smile in time.

'Trust you to find something to laugh about in all of this,' she said.

He took a sip of his brandy. 'It's not really a laughing matter, though, is it?'

'No.' She met his dark eyes. 'It's not.'

'What will you do?'

'Do?' She frowned at him. 'What can I do?'

He put his glass down and folded his arms across his chest as he leant back against the drinks cabinet.

'For a start you could go and speak to Roy Holden.'

'Roy Holden?' Jasmine gaped at him. 'Why? What has he got to do with any of this?'

Connor met and held her startled gaze across the room.

'Because Roy Holden is your father.'

CHAPTER TWELVE

JASMINE genuinely thought she was going to faint. The room spun around her, the sofa opposite intermingling with the tall figure of Connor as he stood watching her reaction to his bombshell.

'My father?' she gasped. *'He's my father?'*

Connor nodded.

'How do you know?' She grasped the nearest surface to anchor herself. 'How can you possibly know that?'

'I found out some time ago.'

She sucked in a painful breath and sat down heavily on the sofa behind her.

'I can't believe it,' she said, almost to herself. 'I can't believe it.'

She felt Connor move across the room to join her on the sofa.

'Does he know?' she asked, turning to look at him.

He nodded. 'Yes. He's known from the start.'

Jasmine buried her head in her lap. She felt the gentle stroke of his hand on her hair and had to fight even harder against the sobs that threatened to consume her.

'I felt a connection with him when I had him as my teacher.' She lifted her tear-stained face towards him. 'I must have known subconsciously at least.'

'Yes.' He threaded his fingers through her hair. 'You must have sensed something.'

'Do you know who my mother was?'

He didn't see any point in denying it now. 'Yes, I do.'

She swallowed deeply, her hands like two tight knots in her lap.

'Who?'

His eyes held hers.

'Your mother was Vanessa Byrne—your aunt.'

Jasmine's jaw dropped.

'My aunt?'

He nodded. 'It seems she had a bit of a rebellious streak and went somewhat off the rails. She was disowned by the family. Her brother, your adopted father Elias, insisted she never darken the doorstep again. When she fell pregnant she was under a lot of family pressure; she finally decided, once you were born, to give you up.'

Jasmine's brow was deeply furrowed as she took it all in. After a long silence she lifted her pained expression to his.

'I found some photographs.' She rummaged in her bag and handed them to him. 'They were in the old Bible at the house.'

He gave the photographs a cursory glance and put them aside. Something in his manner alerted her to the possibility that it wasn't the first time he'd seen them.

'You don't seem very surprised,' she said.

He turned back to face her.

'I'm not.'

'You knew my aunt lived in that house, didn't you?' She stared at him.

He gave a single nod without speaking.

'I...I found a diary as well.' She handed it to him, her voice cracking slightly.

He flipped through the pages, smiling wryly when he came to the lock of hair she'd tucked inside.

'Do you know who gave the photographs and my hair to my aunt?' she asked after a pause.

'I have a fair idea.'

'But you're not going to tell me?'

His eyes came back to hers, his expression regretful.

'It's not my place to tell you.'

'My mother was watching me,' she said after a long silence. 'All those years she was so close and I didn't know.'

'Yes, your intuition was right after all. She was watching you whenever you came past, desperate for a glance at the daughter she'd been forced to give up.'

'I can't believe it.' She sank to the sofa once more. 'It's all so bizarre.'

'Yes, it is certainly that,' he agreed.

'It's so weird.' She lifted her gaze to his. 'Do you know I never realised it till this minute that I've never seen a photograph of my mother?'

'That doesn't surprise me,' he said. 'You were the spitting image of her when she was young. Your parents wouldn't have been able to explain away the likeness, especially as your three sisters are all so alike. From the first, Roy Holden saw it, but assumed it was one of those coincidences. You know, someone having a double somewhere in the world. After a while he stumbled across the truth, but he could do nothing about it. He was married with a child. How could he tell them of a child he hadn't known he'd had? After the scandal he couldn't even clear his own name, let alone yours, without inadvertently revealing the truth.'

Jasmine stared at her hands as she recalled the way it had all blown up in her face. Her favourite teacher blighted by scandal when all the time he was actually her father! He'd done nothing wrong other than listen to a lonely, confused girl who'd felt drawn to his quiet empathetic nature.

When a staff member had interrupted them one afternoon it had all been blown out of proportion. The teacher's aide had scurried off to inform the principal that Jasmine had been in Roy Holden's arms but it hadn't been like that at all. She'd stayed back after class to discuss her English paper with him, only to find herself confessing how unhappy she was over an argument she'd had with her parents that morning. He'd listened as she had off-loaded her frustration, reaching out when the first tears fell to take her hand in his.

The door had opened and they'd sprung apart with unnecessary guilt but it had been too late. It was all over the staff-room by lunchtime and all over the school by the time the home bell sounded. The heightened awareness of inappropriate student-teacher relationships at the time had made it very difficult to stop the hint of a scandal spreading. The climate of suspicion had been too intense to circumvent. Jasmine had watched in mute desperation as exaggerated lie after lie hit the headlines, her total bewilderment leaving deep emotional scars with each fire and brimstone lecture her father had delivered, her devastated mother's distress almost matching her own.

She'd left the school in disgrace and had blamed herself ever since for the damage she'd inadvertently done to Roy Holden's career.

'Does his wife know?' she asked.

'No, he couldn't tell her either without compromising you or your adoptive parents.'

'Secrets everywhere.' Jasmine sighed. 'So many secrets.'

'What will you do?'

'Do?' She looked at him blankly.

'Now that you know the truth, you do have some options.'

'Such as?'

'Such as seeing Roy Holden. You could also insist on finding out more about Vanessa from Elias and Frances.'

'But what about my sisters?'

'What about them?' he asked. 'They need to know the truth as well. I don't think it will harm them all that much. Maybe it will knock a bit of sense into them. Besides, the only one who makes any effort to be worthy of the title sister is Sam.'

'Yes, I know what you mean.' Her tone was wry.

Connor stood up and, draining his brandy, put the empty glass aside.

'You look tired; you should go up to bed. It's been a heck of a day.'

'Yes.' She lowered her gaze from the all-seeing intensity of his. There was still so much she wanted to ask him, like how he knew so much about her family, and things she wanted to tell him but she didn't know where to start.

'I'll sleep in the guest room for the time being,' he said into the telling silence.

'I understand.' She turned away.

'Jasmine?'

She stopped in her tracks and turned back to face him uncertainly.

'I realise this is difficult for you but there are still things we need to discuss,' he said.

'Such as?'

'The future of our marriage.'

'Where were you the last few nights?' she asked, giving him a pointed look.

'I was staying with a friend.'

'Was the friend a woman?'

'Yes, but it was—'

She gave him a chilling glance.

'Our marriage doesn't have a future, Connor.'

His eyes darkened with some indefinable emotion as he took in her simple statement.

'I see.'

'I'm going to bed.' She swung away, frightened he'd see the betraying moisture in her eyes. 'Goodnight.'

He didn't answer but she felt his dark, brooding gaze on her back as she left the room.

The next week passed in a blur of high emotion and recriminations, finally coming to a head when Jasmine confronted Elias and Frances once more. She demanded to see a photograph of her mother and, when they refused, she threatened to go to the press and tell them the whole story.

Elias was under no illusion as to whether or not she meant it.

'I should have known you'd be trouble from the first day

we took you in,' he said through clenched teeth, beads of perspiration sprouting on his receding brow.

'Elias!' Frances gasped.

He gave his wife a dismissive glance before turning back to Jasmine.

'You're on the same path to destruction your poor deluded mother took. I did everything in my power to make her see reason, but she refused to listen.'

'At least she wasn't a hypocrite!' Jasmine threw at him.

'You know nothing of what she put my family through. My parents, your grandparents were never the same again; she destroyed them with her scandalous behaviour.'

'Elias, please.' Frances's voice cracked with a growing anger. 'Vanessa wasn't all that bad.'

He gave her a quelling look but she stood her ground with uncharacteristic defiance.

'You were too hard on her, you know you were,' she continued. 'She wasn't an angel but neither was she the demon you made her out to be.'

'You sent her the photographs, didn't you?' Elias's frown was suddenly accusing.

'Yes,' Frances said with an element of pride in her tone. 'She had the right to see her child, a right you should never have denied her. I also organised for her to stay at the old house so she could at least be close whenever Jasmine went to stay next door.'

'You went behind my back,' Elias said as if he still couldn't quite believe it. 'You deliberately disobeyed my instructions and broke your vow of wifely obedience.'

'Oh, for God's sake, Elias!' Frances got to her feet in agitation. 'I had to do something to heal the hurt before she died.' She turned to Jasmine, her expression softening. 'Darling, your…mother loved you very dearly. I know she did.'

Jasmine could barely make out Frances's features from behind the blur of tears.

'She had an addiction problem she never quite got over.

She tried so hard but her kidneys were permanently damaged. She thought you'd be happier in the long run with us, but maybe…' Her words trailed off as she choked on a sob.

'It's all right.' Jasmine touched her on the arm. 'I understand.'

'It was God's will,' Elias put in gravely. 'All things work together for good.'

'Oh, for Christ's sake, Elias, shut up!' Frances said.

Jasmine couldn't help smiling at the shocked bewilderment on her adoptive father's face. It was certainly a novelty to hear her mother blaspheme but she didn't want to hang around to hear any more. She had more important things to do.

'I have to go,' she said. 'I need to speak to Connor.'

She left after giving them both an awkward hug, knowing it would take much more than a brief show of affection to heal the hurt and misunderstandings that had grown between them. But somehow in that quick embrace she felt something had shifted and settled inside her.

When she returned to Connor's house there was no sign of him having been there recently. She even pushed open the bathroom door to check the floor for towels but the floor was clear. She felt like crying and, just for the heck of it, tore one neatly folded towel from the rail and dropped it to the floor.

She considered asking the housekeeper where he was but changed her mind when she thought about what sort of conclusions Maria would draw, notwithstanding her limited understanding of English.

She wandered aimlessly around the house for a couple of hours when all of a sudden it came to her. She snatched up the keys to the second car and, without even stopping to throw a few things in a bag, rushed out to the garage.

The Friday evening traffic had begun to thin out by the time she hit the freeway and it wasn't all that much after nine p.m. when she pulled up in front of the old house and parked behind Connor's black Maserati.

There were a couple of lights on downstairs and she made

her way to the front door with trepidation in her breast, suddenly uncertain now that she was actually here.

The door was unlocked. She closed it softly behind her and made her way to the nearest door, where a thin beam of light was shining beneath.

The door opened and Connor stood looking down at her, his brows drawn together in a frown.

'What brings you here at this late hour, Jasmine?'

She stepped past him to enter the room, trying not to be too intimidated by his less than enthusiastic greeting.

'I wanted to talk to you about something.' She turned to face him. 'I think you owe me that.'

'Oh, really?' He moved across to the brandy bottle and poured himself a generous measure.

'Yes.'

He took a sip of brandy, holding it in his mouth for a short while before swallowing.

She wasn't sure what to make of his mood.

'I want to know how you came to know Roy Holden was my father.'

He took another sip of brandy before responding.

'Your real mother, Vanessa, told me.'

She stared at him. 'You met my…mother?'

'I met her about three years ago.'

'Where?'

'She was staying at Beryl Hopper's house in the Blue Mountains.'

Jasmine felt her legs weaken and reached for the sofa.

'I was going through a rough time of my own,' he continued. 'I'd just come out of a relationship which had cut me deeply. I landed on Beryl's doorstep as I had done on various occasions in the past. Vanessa was there and we got talking. I can't remember the details exactly but I think I might have mentioned Finn and Sam's relationship. Once she heard the Byrne name she told me of her past, how she had given up her daughter. It didn't take me too long to figure out just which of the Byrne girls she was referring to.'

'You should have told me.'

'How could I?'

'How did you know my mother, I mean Frances, sent the photographs?' she asked.

'Vanessa told me. She also told me Frances had organised for you to have access to the shack at Pelican Head whenever you wanted it.'

Jasmine's mind ran back to all the occasions she'd called her mother's friend to ask if she could use the property. She couldn't recall a single time when it hadn't been immediately available to her.

'I still don't understand.' She lifted her troubled gaze to his. 'Where do you fit in with all this?'

He gave her an unreadable look.

'When I met you first at Finn and Sam's engagement party I couldn't stop myself staring at you. I felt drawn to you even though you kept glaring at me. Vanessa had died a few months earlier, and I guess I wanted to get to know you for her sake, if not for my own. But within a very short time I realised I had rather a task on my hands to win you over. Then we woke up together.'

'So you decided to force me into marrying you?'

He met her scathing gaze.

'Neither knowing Vanessa nor the matter of my mother's estate were the only reasons for marrying you.'

'Oh, really?' Her look was cynical. 'I can just imagine what the other reason might have been! I must have been quite a novelty to you in that I spent a whole night in your bed without throwing myself into your arms.'

'You were certainly a novelty,' he admitted wryly.

'How could you do it, Connor?' Tears sprang to her eyes. 'How could you string me along with such a lie?'

'How could I tell you what I knew?' he asked. 'It wasn't my truth to tell.'

She fought against the tears with difficulty.

'You kept asking me about my family, pointing out the differences all the time. Why did you do that if you were never going to enlighten me?'

He ran a hand through his dark hair.

'I was so close to telling you so many times. It didn't seem fair that you were torturing yourself all the time, hating yourself for being something you could never be. I guess I was hoping you'd come to it yourself. I'm surprised you didn't actually.'

'I think I always knew deep down,' she found herself confessing. 'I just didn't want to come right out and say it.'

'Vanessa was so thrilled that you wanted to work at a drug clinic. It meant the world to her to know you were helping others triumph over the obstacles she never quite managed to overcome. She had no money to speak of, having been cast off by the family, but it pleased her to think you'd developed a social conscience all by yourself.'

'What about the old house?' She frowned at him. 'Didn't she own that?'

He shook his head.

'I bought it a couple of years ago from the person who rented it to her.'

'So then you rented it back to her?'

'No.'

'You let her stay there for nothing?'

Connor shifted his gaze from the tight scrutiny of hers.

'She needed a break. I gave it to her. She found happiness at Pelican Head and a sort of peace.'

She didn't know what to make of this latest development. It was hard to think of Connor being so intimately involved in her life for years without her knowing it.

'Jasmine—' he made a move towards her '—there's something else you need to know.'

Her eyes went to his, her breath suddenly tight in her throat.

'The woman I spent those few nights with was old Beryl

Hopper,' he said. 'I always go there when things get a bit sticky. I was trying to tell you that but I'd only just found out about the unscrupulous dealings of my stepfather over my mother's estate. I guess I wasn't thinking straight so I let you think the worst. I'm sorry.'

Jasmine didn't trust herself to respond without crying.

'I'm not proud of my past,' he continued when she didn't speak. 'I've left a string of broken relationships behind me, flitting from person to person looking for something that up until recently has proved to be elusive.'

She frowned, wondering if she'd missed something.

'When I saw you again at Sam and Finn's wedding I was taken aback. I couldn't stop myself from looking at you all the time; it was as if my whole life I'd been waiting for that moment. It completely rocked me and, I'm ashamed to admit, I hid my reaction behind a cloak of what could only be described as cowardly mockery, when all the time all I felt was the most amazing sense of rightness.'

She blinked up at him in confusion.

'You see, I fell for you the moment you first looked across the church and glared at me.'

'I…I really glared at you?'

He smiled. 'You sure did. I decided then and there I was going to marry you, no matter what. When you turned up in my bed that night I wasn't sure what to do. I know I probably should've woken you and told you of your mistake, but when I saw you curled up in my bed with your beautiful hair spread out over my pillow… Well, it was just too tempting.'

Jasmine couldn't believe her ears.

'I didn't, however, organise the photographer,' he added. 'I had no idea the press would make such a fuss, or indeed your father, or even my stepfather, but when they did it seemed a perfect opportunity to take you out of the firing line by marrying you. I thought that in time you'd get to know me and, hopefully, fall in love with me. I know it was a long shot, but I was desperate.'

'Are you saying what I think you're saying?' she asked.

'What do you think I'm saying?'

'I think you're trying to say what I've wanted to say for ages.'

'Oh?' His chocolate-brown eyes were twinkling and her heart gave a sudden lurch. 'What would that be?'

'I love you.'

He reached for her and enfolded her in his arms, burying his face in her hair.

'I can't believe you just said that.'

Jasmine smiled into the warmth of his chest.

'I can't believe I said it either.'

He put her from him and looked down at her, his eyes dark with desire.

'Do you mean it?'

She crossed her heart with one finger.

'Swear to God and hope to die.'

'I thought you didn't believe in God?' He gave her a mock frown.

She smiled back, her eyes alight with happiness.

'I think I'll give it some further thought,' she said, lifting her mouth for him to kiss.

He grinned as he planted a firm kiss on her up-tilted mouth.

'Thanks be to God,' he said, as once more he gathered her into his arms. 'I love you, Jasmine.'

EPILOGUE

CONNOR put down his paintbrush for the last time and turned to watch Jasmine come up the front steps of the old house.

'Finished?' she asked with a smile.

'Yes, and just in time for me to carry you over the threshold.' He dusted off his hands and reached for her.

'I'm too heavy!' she squealed as he scooped her up.

'And whose fault it that?' He grinned down at her wolfishly.

'Yours,' she said, laying a protective hand over the swell of her belly. 'All yours.'

He kissed her lingeringly before carefully setting her down. 'How are you feeling?'

'I'm fine.' She rested her hands against his chest and smiled up at him. 'I'm just nervous about tomorrow evening.'

'Don't worry, honey,' he reassured her. 'Roy assured me his wife took it all very well. She's just having a little trouble seeing him as a grandfather, that's all.'

Connor had arranged a quiet Christmas celebration at Pelican Head with Elias, Frances, Roy Holden and his wife, Leanne. Jasmine felt touched that he'd gone to so much trouble on her behalf to restore peace and goodwill after months of strained relationships.

'I just hope this baby doesn't make an untimely entrance.' She winced as her belly tightened as it had been doing for the last half hour or so.

'It's not due until New Year,' he reminded her.

'I know but babies often have a mind of their own.'

'Just like their mothers.'

'And their fathers.' She poked at him playfully.

'Yes, but you love me for it, don't you?' he asked with a sexy grin.

'I adore you for it,' she said, pressing a kiss to his neck. 'Even if you still leave your wet towels on the floor all the time.'

'I wouldn't do that if you didn't saunter into the bathroom with absolutely nothing on. I find it distracting, to say the least.'

'But you love me for it, don't you?'

'I adore you for it.' He gathered her closer. 'And you know it.'

Jasmine pressed herself against him for a long moment, breathing in the scent of him, marvelling at how he had turned her life around, filling it with unbelievable love and contentment.

An unmistakable contraction hit her with a sharp jolt.

'Connor?'

'Mmm?' He breathed in the fragrance of her hair.

'Do you think everyone will be upset if they arrive and we're not here?'

Connor lifted her off his chest to look down at her.

'What do you mean we won't be here?' he asked. 'Where else will we be?'

She took his hand and let him feel the contortion of her belly and his eyes widened.

'You mean this is it?'

'I think so.'

'Right now?'

She nodded.

'But what about Christmas? I've bought a turkey!' he exclaimed in panic.

Jasmine laughed.

'I think your baby has decided it wants to celebrate Christmas with us in person.'

'Well, then,' he said, picking up his car keys and taking her arm. 'Let's go see if there's room at the Inn.'

'The Inn?'

'Or, failing that, a stable.' He smiled and gently tapped the end of her nose with one finger. 'And we need to find three wise men and a very bright star.'

She couldn't help giggling at him.

'Connor, you're so irreverent at times.'

'I know.' He winked at her devilishly. 'But I love to see you smile.'

'Why?'

'Because it's heaven on earth, that's why,' he said and kissed her smiling mouth.

Elias and Frances arrived at the old house just as Roy Holden and his wife pulled up. They all went to the front door and peered at the note hastily scrawled there.

Jennifer Vanessa Harrowsmith was born on Christmas Day at five-thirty p.m., six pounds four ounces. Mother and baby doing well, father beside himself. Please help yourself to champagne and nibbles, Oh, and apologise to the turkey—I forgot to tell him he won't be needed this year!

FROM BOARDROOM TO BEDROOM

**Harlequin Presents® brings you two
original stories guaranteed to make
your Valentine's Day extra special!**

THE BOSS'S MARRIAGE ARRANGEMENT
by *Penny Jordan*

Pretending to be her boss's mistress is one thing—but now
everyone in the office thinks Harriet is Matthew Cole's
fiancée! Harriet has to keep reminding herself it's all just
for convenience, but how far is Matthew prepared to go
with the arrangement—marriage?

HIS DARLING VALENTINE
by *Carole Mortimer*

It's Valentine's Day, but Tazzy Darling doesn't care.
Until a secret admirer starts bombarding her with gifts!
Any woman would be delighted—but not Tazzy. There's
only one man she wants to be sending her love tokens, and
that's her boss, Ross Valentine. And her secret admirer
couldn't possibly be Ross...could it?

The way to a man's heart...is through the bedroom

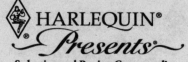

The world's bestselling romance series.

Seduction and Passion Guaranteed!

They're the men who have everything—except a bride....

Wealth, power, charm—what else could a heart-stoppingly
handsome tycoon need? In the GREEK TYCOONS
miniseries you have already been introduced to some
gorgeous Greek multimillionaires who are in need of wives.

THE GREEK BOSS'S DEMAND
by *Trish Morey*
On sale January 2005, #2444

THE GREEK TYCOON'S CONVENIENT MISTRESS
by *Lynne Graham*
On sale February 2005, #2445

THE GREEK'S SEVEN-DAY SEDUCTION
by *Susan Stephens*
On sale March 2005, #2455

Pick up a Harlequin Presents® novel and you will enter a world
of spine-tingling passion and provocative, tantalizing romance!

Available wherever Harlequin books are sold.

www.eHarlequin.com

If you enjoyed what you just read,
then we've got an offer you can't resist!

Take 2 bestselling love stories FREE!

Plus get a FREE surprise gift!

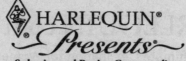